C000245718

Back in the USSR

By the same author

HUNTER DAVIES

Back in the USSR

Ещё Раз ь СССР

Hamish Hamilton London

First published in Great Britain 1987
by Hamish Hamilton Ltd
27 Wrights Lane   London W8 5TZ

Copyright © 1987 by Amnesty International

British Library Cataloguing in Publication Data
Davies, Hunter
Back in the USSR
1. Soviet Union—Description and
Travel—1970-
914.7'04854   DK29
ISBN 0-241-12328-3

Phototypeset by Pioneer
Perthshire   Scotland
Printed and bound by Butler and Tanner Ltd
Frome and London

With a little help from my friends,
Margaret and Flora . . .

Contents

July 17th 1986   EXPECTATIONS Before we Went

Grey was the colour - grey crowds, grey
clothes, grey streets, everything sombre & grim,
1940's impression of austerity, queues, nothing in the
shops at the end of the queues, virtually no cars,
armed police everywhere, people unsmiling &
suspicious if not hostile .... But then that
got confused as an image after Chernobyl when
on tele the Kiev people looked so happy,
colourful & modern. As a taxi driver sd: to me
"they can't have drafted in that many actors
to fool people." Maybe it isn't so grey after
all. Still expect awful food, a general ugliness,
no adverts. In Georgia images from novels
keep coming in — jolly old peasants doing
dopey dances & flinging vodka glasses over
their shoulder, lots of singing & shouting,
big, black haired / bearded men etc.

Most of all I expect to wonder how people
can live like this — expect to be aware of
them not being free to express themselves,
of not enjoying many of the luxuries of
life, of feeling constrained & frustrated.
Can't imagine how I think this will express
itself or how I'll sense it.

Can't believe half the things we've been
told to take will really be necessary — will

Expectations of Russia...

Can only be found from the
images formed from "white
nights", documentures, and the
obvious Russian spy stories —
where every one wears square fur
hats and is Grey, fat and
weather beaten ".

So I then expect Moscow to be
Cold, dead and full of large Grey
buildings which I hope is not
true ". I imagine everybody
to be very old fashioned in
clothing and appearance, full
of old sad looking, dumpy
women and fat, boring middle-
age executive men. I have no
idea of what Russian youth
will be like apart from the
well known eagerness of pos-
essing western clothes,
records, labels etc.
      I think the food will ↝

CHAPTER ONE

Getting Ready

Thoughts and expectations on leaving . . .

They will be grim and cheerless, at least in Moscow. They will be repressed and be suspicious of us and each other. The KGB will be watching us, and them, all the time. We will be bugged. I might even be led into a compromising situation. That could be fun. Naked girls assaulting me in our hotel bedroom and then flash, it's all been recorded on photograph.

They will be after my jeans, such a shame I don't wear them any more, not since I got over forty years old and reached a 34-inch waist. Should I go to Marks and buy a pair? To give as a present of course, not to sell. I wouldn't dare do that. I'd be arrested straightaway.

I expect them to be humourless. There weren't many laughs in Dostoevsky when I read him last, back in the sixth form. Perhaps I missed the jokes, just as you can miss the fun in Dickens, if you're a foreigner. And all those long names. Will Russians really address each other all the time as Ivan Ivanovich? Surely in real life they have short nicknames.

1

It will all look horrible, an architectural wilderness, nasty buildings, tatty shops. I've only been behind the Iron Curtain once and that was to Bucharest in 1972 when I was doing a book about Tottenham Hotspur. The hotel was modern and plush, like a Hilton, with all mod cons, such as prostitutes wandering round the corridors at night, quite openly, looking for customers, using funny old English phrases such as 'Do you like me?' I don't think any of the Spurs were taken in, but then they can get all that at home.

Will we make friends in Russia? Will they be too scared? The educated ones will be interested in the West, because they would really like to escape from repression at home and get away. That's why they are kept in, not allowed out. Well, that's what most of us in the West believe. The media tell us so. Must be true.

They will be very boring. What a generalisation, how can you say such a thing about a vast country, the biggest in the world? There will be non-boring people, but they won't be allowed to be non-boring in our presence. I've seen how boring they can be in London. The Soviet Trade Delegation has its monster residential block near us in Highgate, and there are also several local private houses which they have taken over. I watch them trudging across the Heath, carrying their plastic bags, coming back from Kentish Town with their shopping, in their old-fashioned clothes, old-fashioned hair. The minute you get within eye contact, or earshot, they stop talking, never smile at you, yet I know many of their faces by now, and they must know me. Are they *told* not to smile, or is that really their nature?

Flora had several Russians in her class at Brookfield Primary, when she was about seven. In fact for a whole year she used to speak in a pretend Russian-language gobbledegook she had created, which she could keep up for ages. It sounded quite genuine, as she had picked up the tones and sounds of her Russian friends talking to each other, but of course it was all rubbish, like the Swedish chef on the Muppets speaking pretend Swedish. When we asked what she was speaking, she would answer 'South Russian'. She can't remember any of it now. But how strange that after all these years we should be taking her to the genuine South Russia. Does Georgia count as South Russia? I must mug up my geography before we leave.

There will be lots of queues. I will have to drink a lot of vodka. There will be no sink plugs.

Right, I think that's most of the preconceptions and stereotypes cleared from my mind. I'll now ask my good wife Margaret and my younger daughter Flora if they will be kind enough to write down their pre-Russian thoughts, uncluttered by any facts, untainted by any experiences. Once you arrive in a new place, you forget what you thought beforehand.

I hope to persuade both Margaret and Flora to keep a diary during our Russian travels. Lucky Flora, aged thirteen. At her age, I hadn't been further south than Penrith.

Expectations before we went

Margaret • • • Grey was the colour – grey crowds, grey clothes, grey streets, everything sombre and grim, 1940s impression of austerity, queues, nothing in the shops at the end of the queues, virtually no cars, armed police everywhere, people unsmiling and suspicious if not hostile. . . . But then that got confused as an image when on tele last night the Kiev people looked so happy, colourful and modern. As a taxi driver said to me 'they can't have drafted in *that* many actors to fool people'. Maybe it isn't so grey after all. Still, expect awful food, a

3

general ugliness, no adverts. In Georgia images from novels keep coming in – jolly old peasants doing dopey dances and flinging vodka glasses over their shoulder, lots of singing and shouting, big, black-haired/bearded men, etc.

Most of all I expect to wonder how people can live like this – expect to be aware of them not being free to express themselves, of not enjoying many of the luxuries of life, of feeling constrained and frustrated. Can't imagine how I think this will express itself or how I'll sense it.

Can't believe half the things we've been told to take will really be necessary – will we need sink plugs/loo paper? It's all silly I'm sure. Will everything we say be bugged? Will we know? Will we be able to wander freely or really have a minder?

I'm *not* looking forward to:
the Moscow hotel,
the food there,
the lack of real freedom to wander at will,
any of us being ill,
I *am* looking forward to:
feeling this is really different,
the Kremlin and Red Square,
Gorky Park, all parks,
an old-fashioned orchestra-playing restaurant,
an old-fashioned sea-side feel in Georgia,
actually talking to Russians,
seeing my *Thackeray* in Russian,
anti-feminism in operation,
the Metro.

I'm surprisingly pro-Russian in feeling – certainly not frightened of them/it. But I have to struggle to remember this *is* the country that imprisons writers and Jews, that has the KGB, that won't let its people travel freely in and out. I tend only to see Russia in a romantic way, heavily influenced by the classic novels rather than the modern ones • • •

Expectations of Russia . . .

Flora • • • Can only be found from the images formed from the film *White Nights*, from documentaries, and the obvious Russian spy stories – where everyone wears square fur hats and is grey, fat and weatherbeaten.

So I then expect Moscow to be cold, dead and full of large grey buildings which I hope is not true. I imagine everybody to be very old-fashioned in clothing and appearance, full of old sad-looking, dumpy women and fat, boring, middle-aged executive men. I have no idea of what Russian youth will be like, apart from the well-known eagerness to possess Western clothes, records, labels, etc.

I think the food will be horrible with a lack of Vitamin C, just undercooked red meat and vodka.

That is the only expectation I can think of which I hope will be entirely wrong.

I have absolutely no image of Georgia, except that the name Black Sea sounds cold, dark and mysterious • • •

Six Months Before

The invitation came out of the blue. I got a message one day from someone called Mr Roberts from something called the Great Britain-USSR Association to ask if I'd like a holiday in Russia. It was the word 'holiday' which attracted me.

Over the years, Margaret and I have had invitations from official bodies to go abroad with groups of other British writers, but we've never gone. We didn't like the idea of leaving the children behind. We didn't like the idea of official tours. They maintain of course that you see much more when it's official, and you have good times, especially when people like Beryl Bainbridge are in your party, getting drunk and dancing on tables. Michael

5

Holroyd, Margaret Drabble, Penelope Lively, Fay Weldon, Melvyn Bragg and a dozen or so others who have carried our banners to foreign fields all say it's very interesting. But they have to give lectures, listen to endless talks from other writers, join conferences, prepare papers. It's the thought of smoke-filled rooms in some crummy hotel in some People's Republic, listening to their official spokesmen all day, which has always put me off.

But a *holiday* sounded more attractive. We have enough holidays each year, and why not? What's the point of working so hard? But it might be nice to go somewhere unusual for a change, and to have someone else organising it. I do tire of being responsible for plane tickets, these last twenty-five years of married life.

So I rang Mr Roberts, a very puckah-sounding, rather clipped gentleman, and asked him for more details. Yes, it would be a holiday, a family holiday. The Russians wanted a writing couple, man and woman, to go with their family to spend a holiday with Russian writers and their families, on their holidays. Apparently, if you're in the Writers Union, one of the perks is a cheapo holiday by the seaside every year. It would be a unique opportunity, a chance to get to know Russians informally, on their holidays, not in an official setting.

I asked, why me? Did he expect me to do a BBC programme about Russia? (At the time, I was still doing *Bookshelf* on Radio 4.) Did he think Margaret might get a novel out of it? Or were they just hoping for a nice mention in *Punch*? No, there were no strings attached. We didn't have to do anything while we were there, apart from enjoy ourselves, nor write or do anything afterwards. The Russians simply liked the idea of the *presence* of a Western writing family, sharing a holiday with their own writers.

And, er, well, Mr Roberts, will it be free? Of course. You will be their guests. Just as their writers are our guests when they come here. I asked him to put it on paper, just in case it was some smart bugger playing tricks.

I examined the notepaper when it came, wondering what the 'Q' in 'J. C. Q. Roberts' might mean. I looked him up in *Who's Who* and found it stood for Quentin. He went to King's College, Taunton, and then Oxford. He's been a master at Marlborough and worked for many years round the world for Shell. Since 1974, he's been director of the Great Britain-USSR Association. Could that be the cover biog. for a spy? He's been in a lot of far-flung places in his Shell career, from Kenya to Vienna. I wondered what he was really doing there. And on whose side.

Margaret was suspicious. Not because of who or what might be putting up the money, but because we would end up being beholden. She has never taken a free thing in her life, unlike me in my *Sunday Times* days when you worked hard to get a free trip from a PR company. It's their job to get journalists on free things, and the job of journalists to take, but not get taken in. That's the way the world works, in the West. But Margaret has led a rather sheltered life.

Look, this bloke Roberts has to find writers to send out there. I believe him when he says there are no strings. What can they gain from little old us anyway? When their lot come here, they get paid for by the GB-USSR, which probably means our Government, which means in the end *we* pay. We're not taking it from some dodgy commercial firm. This is legit.

Yes, she said, but there's no such thing as a free glass of vodka. You'll have to pay, some way. You'll see.

Three Months To Go . . .

I never thought at my age that I would ever be called upon to learn something completely new. I haven't mastered the old tricks yet, so what would I want with any extra ones? Learning anything gives me such a headache. I've no sooner got today's date in my head, than they go and change it. It will never come back. All that effort for nothing.

Yet, every Thursday at 5.30, the three of us have been leaving our front door, turning left down the street, each of us carrying our books, our pads, our pens, our folders. Three swots all, off for our weekly lesson.

What on earth can they be doing? think the neighbours. Yes, I've noticed them as well. Every Thursday, at the same time, for the last five weeks. Have the Davieses gone potty? Have they joined a secret sect? I say, gang, let's follow them.

And so, like three Pied Pipers, we step out, watched by the nosey-parkers of the neighbourhood, the nosiest ones dodging behind trees to get a better gape. We take the second left and knock on the door of Barbara, our esteemed teacher. Knock, knock, we knock. When you're learning anything new, there's a hell of a lot of repetition.

I usually allow the two women members of our party to take the lead, letting them stride along the street ahead of me, looking trim and terribly important. More often than not I'm shouting, 'Hold on, wait for me!' as I stumble out of the door, trying to catch them, at the same time attempting to do some last-minute homework. Okay then, first-minute homework. They're such creeps, those two.

We three, we happy three, are learning Russian. We go in three months, all being well. Now that the paperwork seems to be progressing, it was suggested it would be only courteous to our hosts to try and learn a bit of their language. You must be joking. Don't we have interpreters, taking us to everything, from queue to queue, round every collective farm? I've seen the films.

Actually, we might find it surprisingly luxurious. It is a very nice beach, so they say, pretty scenery, just like the best of the Mediterranean.

Perhaps I've got a gift I never knew I had. Could this be my hidden talent, the one I've gone through life hoping for? Each time, as a child, when I took up a new thing such as the violin, or cricket, or semaphore in the Boy Scouts, I thought this is it, maybe I'll be a Natural. It always seemed so unfair, when you looked around at other kids. Some could pick up a pencil and bingo, they drew a face that looked like a face, or be taught a new ball game and instantly be brilliant at it, or pick up a new instrument and manage a tune. There must be *something*, just waiting for me to come along. Still looking.

I know now, after only four weeks, that it won't be Russian. I've done better than Jake. He moaned on for years, waiting to start German at school, convinced he was going to be terrific, after all those war comics he'd been reading, having mastered *svinehund* and *blitzen*. In just two weeks he knew he'd never make it.

Like so many absolute beginners, I have lashed out on the gear, buying the BBC instructional course, which comes with three whopping cassettes and a teach-yourself book, thinking I'll quickly get so far ahead, I'll be teaching the teacher. I haven't got the time, that's the real reason.

As for those two teacher's pets, I don't talk to them, mainly because they just ignore me; who is this dum-dum at the back of the class, keeping us all back? Margaret does at least fifteen minutes every morning, sitting on her own in the kitchen.

Flora does her bit each evening in her own room, which is pretty good, considering she also has her normal homework. She's got a terrific accent already.

It was the same when I was sent to those violin lessons.

I did nothing till ten minutes before each lesson, then I either came over sick and said, I can't go, mam, send him a note, I feel ever so poorly, or I quickly tried to do what I was supposed to have practised during the week, all in five minutes. Being there, at the actual lesson, I quite enjoyed that. Same with the Russian. In the lesson itself, time passes quickly and I appear to be learning.

Go on, ask me any letter of the alphabet, just as long as they're the easy ones, such as what's A in Russian? or what's K? I know both of those. Mainly because they're the same as in English. Can't teach me.

But the rest of them, gee whizz. St Cyril has a lot to answer for. His Cyrillic alphabet is utterly potty. I'd just mastered the fact that the Russians write our letter 't' as an 'm', but when they print it, as opposed to handwriting it, it becomes a T. What the hell are they playing at? And why is our P your R and our B your V? You really should sort yourselves out, chaps.

Then, of course, there's all those strange squiggles, those funny shapes, which bear no relation to anything we use. Margaret sits every morning writing them out. She's fallen in love with the shapes, and loves copying them, almost as a drawing lesson. Flora loves the sound of Russian. Margaret loves the look. What I like best of all is when Barbara says *dasveedanya*. That means goodbye.

As another preparation, we have started reading background books, but what a trouble we've had getting any. I went to our local bookshop, the High Hill in Hampstead, where the young man on the travel section was very helpful. He recommended Colin Thubron's *Among the Russians*, a snip from Penguin at £3.95, and *Life in Russia* by Michael Binyon, from Granada at £2.95. He wasn't quite sure about the actual guide books. I had a look at them, such as they were, and could see nothing suitable. As a guide book writer, if only to the Lake District, I enjoy looking at guides to places I know nothing about, just to see how they've organised themselves, if they make sense to the complete beginner. Most of the books were on Leningrad and Moscow. I could see nothing on Georgia, which was what I wanted. In the end I bought Fodor's *Soviet Union*, as it looked as if some real research had been done, though I'm not usually a fan of the Fodor guides. But the price, *mon dieu*, just for a paperback – £12.95. Well, the trip is free. I hope.

We also started reading all the newspaper stories about Russia. Once you know you're going somewhere new, the name seems to jump out and hit you in the eye all the time. Martin Walker in the *Guardian* seemed to be the best, getting into normal Russian life. I made a note to write to him, when our details were definite. We still didn't have them.

There was a piece in the *Sunday Times* by the editor, Andrew Neil, on his first visit, full of the usual stuff about Russia, the privileges of the top party bosses, with their big posh cars, tearing down the middle of the roads. I could have written it without ever having been to Russia. He appeared to have seen only what he had set out to see beforehand. Yet how can I know the truth?

It's strange how in just a few months I have become protective of Russia, just by starting to learn their language, getting to know a little about their country, feeling sorry for them when the old prejudices still get trotted out. It's not necessarily deliberate political bias. Journalists get taken in by themselves, just as much as other people do. I've talked to footballers after a match who actually say they're as sick as a parrot, because they've read in newspapers that that's what players say. And burglars, when caught, really do say it's a fair cop. Clichés perpetuate themselves.

One Month To Go . . .

Three things have happened to give us second thoughts. We're now seriously wondering whether we should cancel. Is it wise, is it prudent, will it be pleasurable?

Our first doubts were caused by the Round Table. This was a meeting in London last month organised by the GB-USSR Association to which Margaret and I were invited, as part of the British team, to debate certain topics with a party of visiting Russian writers.

That's it, she said. I knew there would be a catch. Even before we've been, we will have to sing for our supper. This will go on for ever now, being invited to dreary meetings. And, once we've actually *taken* their hospitality, we will be committed for always.

The Round Table topics did sound particularly dreary. 'Are Traditional Human Values threatened by urbanisation and other phenomena in contemporary society and how is this reflected in literature?' Dear God, what a mouthful. Bags me not take part in that one. The other subject was slightly better. 'Is nostalgia for the past a positive or a negative phenomenon in literature?'

I went to one session and throughout it the Russians banged away at two main points, neither relevant. How our punks were disgusting, a mark of our decadent, druggie capitalist society. How Russia had lost twenty million people in the War, a fact we in the West don't seem to realise.

Later, over drinks, the Russians did not seem quite as grim. They must have been given brief biogs. on us, just as we had been given stuff on them, because during the evening three of them came up and asked if I had any Beatles photographs or badges. As usual, no one was interested in my wonderful Wordsworth biography or my great George Stephenson book. Just the Fab Four.

I also met a lady called Svetlana, who I thought at first

12

was one of the translators. She looked about sixty, small and sharp with eagly eyes, very quick, very good English. John said she was important, so I should talk to her about our forthcoming trip, but be careful.

I wasn't sure what this meant. Had I not to say what a boring load of old farts you've brought to London, which would, of course, be impolite. Or was she KGB and had I to beware as she might try to use me somehow?

She said she was from the Writers Union in Moscow and she had already arranged a translator-guide for us in Moscow, a calm Jewish girl who would suit me very well. She looked at me and smiled. I took that to mean that an over-active, noisy, rushing-around person needed calmness. Very true. She also gave me the name of the place we were going to on the Black Sea and I got her to write it down – Pitsunda.

It was the first time it all seemed real, that we really would be going to Russia. Up to now, I half felt John had made it up, and that no one in Moscow had the slightest knowledge of our impending arrival.

'And what would you like to do in Moscow?' she said. 'What are your interests?'

I couldn't decide whether it was just idle chat, something to say to me at the party, or she meant it.

'Not the Bolshoi Ballet,' I said. 'No theatres at all. No tractor farms.'

I trotted out the first things that came into my head, thinking they would be completely ignored. They will take us to what they always take visitors to. That's their system.

'Then what would you like to see?'

'Well, I think a disco would be nice for Flora, and I'd like to see a football match. Oh, and how about a train ride to the Black Sea, rather than a plane? I do love trains. Have you read my book . . . ?'

Next day, Margaret went along to her Round Table

13

session, where once again the Russians managed to drag the war into every discussion. And, if not the war, then it was punks. This time John Roberts had brought along a *Sunday Times* colour mag, which showed photographs of punks with their parents.

Margaret did not find the drinks afterwards all that interesting, which I had done, but she passed on my little packages. I had shoved a few Beatles photos and stuff in various envelopes, marking them Vitaly, Yuri and Svetlana. As she handed them over, each person carefully looked round the room, then quickly shoved their envelope in their inside pocket, without saying anything.

She came home depressed by all the Russians she'd listened to. Not only were they grey and humourless, obsessed by the war, they were also sexist. She had asked why there were no women in their party of writers and they had made silly jokes, such as our women are at home in the kitchen, where they should be.

Do we really want to go and spend our precious summer holidays with such awful people? If those eight writers are the cream, what will the rest be like? We could be stuck with hundreds of them, in some godforsaken spot on the Black Sea, with absolutely no escape.

Our second cause for concern was more serious. From the beginning, we had worried if we should go to a country which had political prisoners and victimised Jews, but we had rationalised it by saying it would be valuable to see Russia from the inside, to have first-hand experience of some aspects of their life, however limited it might be.

Through the post came a book about Irina Ratushinskaya called *No I'm not Afraid*. A covering note said she was 'the most important Russian writer of her generation'. In 1983, she was sentenced to seven years' hard labour. 'Her crime: writing poetry.' I had never heard of her before, or her case, but the documentary evidence in the book was frightening, showing how she had been ill-treated and persecuted.

I then saw a review of it in the *Sunday Times* by Freddy Raphael in which he attacked people who went on 'sponsored trips to the Soviet Union, so reluctantly and so regularly . . . if the devil keeps a good enough table, there will always be those who can find excuses to dine with him'.

What a dilemma. Can we really excuse ourselves if we go? If only we were paying, my conscience might be slightly salved, but then if we went as Thomson tourists we wouldn't get inside the Black Sea writers' homes. If we do meet their top writers, I will bring up the subject of Irina, and protest about her treatment. Is that an acceptable stance? Oh, such a worry. We never have these moral problems when we go to the Lake District.

Then the third thing happened, the most worrying of all: Chernobyl. Since May, when we all first heard about the nuclear power station disaster, the news seemed to get worse every day, people being evacuated round Kiev, fresh fruit being banned in Poland, clouds of poison reaching Western Europe.

We studied maps again. We hadn't been able to find Pitsunda, but presumed it must be in the Crimea, which is roughly south of Kiev, the most dangerous area. Oh, no.

All our neighbours said that's it, you won't be going now, surely not. Not with Flora, a young girl. You might not know for decades if she had been affected, till she has children herself.

I wrote to John Roberts, for guidance, but he was away. The news was so contradictory. There had been an American story that suggested 20,000 had been killed.

Now the Russians were reporting that only twenty or so had died, though more were on the danger list.

A Scottish radio reporter from Aberdeen came to interview Margaret about Bonny Prince Charlie and she happened to mention our forthcoming Russian trip. Should we cancel? He came out with a mass of facts and figures about radiation, all very impressive, as he had made a study of Dounreay. He said all the air in the world was now radioactive. It didn't matter where you went, you would be breathing it. One place was really not much more dangerous than another. He couldn't see why Moscow was worse than London. In fact the Lake District was probably worse than either – and that's where we normally spend three months of every year. In the Lake District, the lambs were now radioactive.

We still wavered and fretted, and in the end it was William Whitelaw, Denis Healey and David Owen, who finally decided us. Just a few weeks before we were due to go, they went on some official delegation to Moscow and saw Mr Gorbachev. If it's safe for them, we thought it must be OK for us. Willie Whitelaw is a national treasure. They wouldn't risk him.

I heard Mr Healey on the Radio talking about the huge advances they had made, how Gorbachev was bringing in great improvements, life was suddenly becoming freer, officialdom more open. The fact that they had owned up immediately to Chernobyl, made all the information available at once, was remarkable, given the normal Russian reaction to bad news.

Now, so they all seemed to say, was the best time for many, many years to visit Russia. Enormous changes were going on. It was exciting just to be there, and see what was happening. Gorbachev, according to all the newspapers, even the right-wing ones, was making huge strides. Russia, at this moment, was an exciting place to be . . .

16

CHAPTER TWO

Getting There

We were checking in at London Airport when this person-checker said heh, there's a message coming through on the computer for you. Oh no, I thought, not problems already. The Russians don't know we are coming, our tickets are not valid, MI6 want to see us before we go, or it's the KGB, wanting to know exactly what I gave Svetlana.

The previous week I got a strange message from the British Embassy in Moscow, passed on by John Roberts. Svetlana had been mugged near Victoria station and her handbag stolen, just after the Round Table conference. In her bag was my unopened envelope. Could I supply details of what was in it? John burst out laughing when I said two Beatles photos and a Sergeant Pepper badge. That was all? No letter? Nope, nothing else. He accordingly informed Moscow.

The person-checker studied her computer and then told us what the message said. We were all being invited to the Executive Lounge. Have a nice flight.

I'd never heard of an Executive Lounge at Heathrow. Were the Russians already trying to soften us up? It took some finding as it was hidden behind a dull-looking door I must have passed dozens of times over the years, fighting my way through the crowds to the duty free. Inside, it was very posh, like a high-class hotel, with some very sleek receptionists. I gave our names and the sleekest one said oh yes, you are guests of Geoffrey Felton.

I caught the word guest, and immediately started helping myself to the stuff on offer, I know how guests should behave, but I could not place the name of our host. Flora and I inspected the drinks, the big colour TV, the comfy sofas, but Margaret refused to look at anything. There's obviously some mistake she said. In that case, let's enjoy ourselves before they find out.

An impressive-looking chap in full BA uniform, masses of ribbon, nice hair, said hello, Hunter, I'm Geoffrey. I looked into his physog, desperately peeling away the decades, unravelling the layers of life, and gradually saw a little lad I think I used to terrorise on our council estate in Carlisle, back in the early Fifties. Not *that* Geoffrey Felton.

He's now a Dispatcher, whatever that is, but obviously quite grand. He had seen our names on the passenger list. Very observant. He then asked for our boarding tickets and took them away. Very strange. He reappeared later in the boarding lounge and returned them. They were now first class tickets. Wasn't that kind.

BA flight 710 to Moscow on July 18, 1986 seemed practically empty, which was presumably why Geoffrey had been able to give us better seats. Out of thirty first class spaces, I counted only five passengers. I didn't look in the economy section. Let them count themselves.

The night before, I'd spoken to Mark Lefanu, Secretary of the British Society of Authors. I'd asked him about his recent Moscow visit and whether he had enjoyed it. No, he said, enjoy was not the word he would use about Russia. 'It was an experience.'

He suggested that as presents we should take little things like biros or postcards. Other people suggested electrical stuff, such as pocket calculators, cheap digital watches. John Roberts said no sink plugs, no need to take them, not in modern Russian hotels. This whole thing about sink plugs had been based on a misconception. It isn't that Russian plumbing is so ancient and inefficient that they don't have sink plugs. It's because they don't *want* sink plugs. Russians consider it rather dirty to wash yourself in stagnant water. You keep the mixer tap running and the water fresh, if you're shaving or washing your hands. In London, John is always getting complaints from Russians who have burned their hands.

We had a whole load of presents with us on the plane, many of which I can't quite remember the reasons for. On our holiday in Moscow, we took with us, wait for it, five pairs of tights, three Mary Quant make-up sets to be given by Flora to any friends she made, five packs of felt pens for any younger children, two bottles of whisky, twenty postcards showing punks, twenty postcards showing the Royal Family, let's keep it balanced, two of Margaret's novels, three of my books, five glossy magazines, two packets of tea, two packets of coffee, twenty copies of *Beatles Monthly*, twenty-four cheap razors for taxi drivers, two copies of *Punch*, and a Fergie and Prince Andrew souvenir mug, destination unknown.

We had discovered, by a great coincidence, that Margaret's biography of Thackeray, published in Britain several years ago, was that week going to come out in Russia. We'd been given the name of her Moscow publisher, and told to contact him. I had the name of a Russian publisher, interested in doing my Beatles biog., so I had a copy for him. I'd packed a pile of *Beatles Monthlies* at the last moment, presuming Russians would like such stuff. These are the 1960s fan mags, full of photographs, and now collector's items, though the ones I was taking were mostly facsimile copies. Well, the Russians will never tell the difference.

The champagne flowed freely the moment we got on

board, and I graciously accepted a couple perhaps even three. The lunch was excellent and we were given a choice of main course. One of the hostesses, knowing I was a friend of the very important Mr Felton, pressed five little bottles of wine upon me, saying I could find them useful in Moscow.

Margaret got talking to a gentleman three seats away from her, very impressive chap in a dark striped suit. I talked to him later and he turned out to be the Ghana Ambassador to Moscow. He'd been there three years, with his wife and three children, one of whom was at Moscow University. There are 1,000 Ghanaian students in Moscow who live in hostels, always with a Russian sharing their quarters. 'They find it very cold.' Some people found Moscow boring, but the ballet and the theatre were his hobby, so he enjoyed it.

He'd been passing through London, returning from Accra to Moscow. We discussed the Commonwealth Games, which were beginning that week in Edinburgh. He said Ghana had just backed out, because of Mrs Thatcher's attitude to sanctions. It was a shame. 'We have some good girl sprinters. Not gold material, but perhaps a bronze.'

In Moscow, he often has to go to three diplomatic parties a day. If I rang him in Moscow, he would invite me to one. He got out his card and gave it to me, John Tettegah. 'Our parties are very popular with Russians. We have drink at our parties, you see,' he said with a smile.

I'd always thought the diplomatic world floated on drink, so what was surprising about that? Anyway, the Writers Union will be looking after us in Moscow. No need to impose ourselves on the Ghanaians.

We were now nearing Moscow. I wrote a quick post-card to Margaret's father in Carlisle, 85-year-old Arthur. He does like to know where we are. We'd been told phone calls to Britain were impossible and that postcards could take months, if they ever arrived at all. I datelined it Moscow-ish, and persuaded the air hostess to post it back in London.

She'd just been telling us once again that no photographs are allowed while flying over Soviet territory. I could see nothing at all through the clouds. I wasn't going to waste my Olympus Trip on them, even if they were Russian clouds.

M. • • • A pity the plane was BA. It didn't feel like going to Russia. Hunt in ecstasies 'cos an old neighbour from Carlisle got us into the executive lounge and then 1st Class tickets – he loved it, he loved it – and how the stewardess spoiled and fussed over him, but as the plane was just about empty it wasn't hard. Best bit was chatting to the ambassador to Moscow from Ghana – huge black man in pin-striped suit and sparkling shirt who at first seemed v. formidable but once he got going had the jolliest smile and great laugh. He told me he'd been in prison five years till a new General took over but as he was a trade union man and all the officials in prison were in unions he did quite well. Confirmed worst suspicions that Moscow *was* dry. I don't think Hunt realises the situation yet • • •

We queued up for Passport Control at Moscow Airport and I could sense Flora becoming slightly alarmed. It was quite scary, standing on your own, under strong lights, being examined intently by a uniformed militiaman, while he accusingly looked you up and down and consulted forms. There were mirrors everywhere, so he could see all of you, front and back, presumably to check your height and personal details. Perhaps that was why Flora was getting worried. Since filling in her passport form last year, she's put on about three inches, gone from brunette to blonde and looks about twenty-three rather than thirteen. He might suspect something.

I started to giggle, but then I'd had three, okay, maybe four glasses of champagne. The whole palaver was no doubt meant to intimidate the foreign visitor, but I began to realise that the militiaman was in reality a spotty youth, fresh from the sticks, straight from Carlislsky, probably more scared than Flora, knowing that he was being watched by unseen eyes, to see that he did his job properly.

We all got through okay, and in fact we picked up our baggage and were out of the airport in only half an hour, a world record for us. At Easter in San Francisco it had taken two hours. From then on I kept on thinking, is this normal, or are they doing it for us?

Our Minder was lovely, Marina, aged about thirty, gentle and calm. I do tend to get frantic when travel arrangements go wrong, but they couldn't this time, hurrah, as I was not in charge. I think all family holidays should be done this way. Fathers need a break. I'd like a minder through life, please.

We drove into Moscow and Marina pointed out the memorial on the city boundary, marking the spot where the Germans were stopped in the last war. Russia lost twenty million in that war, are you listening, Flora, this trip is supposed to be educational.

We were booked into the Ukraine Hotel. It was unbelievable. It looked like a giant cathedral, a monster St Pancras station, with twenty-nine floors and 1,500 rooms. There are five other giant buildings, all the same design, ringed round Moscow, built on Stalin's orders in the 1950s as part of his plan to show that Russians can build skyscrapers too, you know.

We had a suite of rooms, plush and elegant enough, but 1950s plush, with red satinette covers on the sofas, just like my mother used to have. It even had a piano, dreadfully out of tune, but just imagine, a piano in a hotel bedroom.

Hold on, I said, could be bugged. Chandeliers are old hat by now, every reader of spy novels knows that. Be very careful what you say in front of that piano, Flora.

I was longing to be bugged, longing to think of some poor sod trying to work out what the hell our stupid family arguments might be about. But why would they bother with us? Such self-importance. I suppose Russian visitors to the West have the same fantasies, brought up on the same rubbish as we are.

There was a huge colour TV, and Flora at once had it tuned in to what looked like *Top of the Pops*, circa 1976, while I went hunting for a sink plug. There wasn't one! At last, one of the clichés had come true. Margaret pronounced the lav paper unusable, except as sandpaper, so that made two. Then we went in search of refreshments.

We'd arranged to meet Svetlana in the buffet which was just along the corridor. Every floor has its own buffet. Svetlana looked younger than she did in London and was probably my age. Quite a young woman in other words. And she was more important than I had first imagined, being head of the English section of the Writers Union in Moscow.

Svetlana outlined all the excitements ahead. We were to have a whole week in Moscow, which was news to us, and they had organised events for every day, though we didn't have to do anything we didn't want to. She gave us each a neat typewritten itinerary, in English, all very efficient. I could see quite a few dinner parties on the list, which looked good, plus sightseeing to places I'd never heard of. The biggest surprise was that there, on the itinerary, were the words Football Match and also the word Disco. I nudged Flora, but she was busy doing something with her sausage. She hadn't passed many comments on Russia so far, nor had Margaret.

F. • • • Touched down at around 4.30 (Russian time). Stood for ages while Passport Control sat and stared at you, making you stand and glare back at him so he could check suspiciously your height, looking around at the mirrors that surrounded me.

Met Marina and proceeded in a cab on a long wide main road completely straight that led all the way to the Centre (so called) of Moscow. Looking out either side of the Taxi the surroundings looked disappointingly like GB, flat green fields and trees, etc. Approaching Moscow itself, I could see just polished-looking numerous white tower blocks rising in the flat landscape in clusters. Hotel is named (after straining to pronounce the weird writing that looked utter gibberish) 'The Guesthouse Ukraine'. It rises twenty-nine floors high in beige sandstone looking like an English cathedral with a huge spire. It's on the bank of the 'Moskva' river (which looks as drab as the Thames).

Our passports were checked and double-checked just to get through reception, then on each floor a woman stares at you seated at a little desk with a lamp. Known as 'the lady of the floor', it is she who takes your room keys and gives you little identity cards so you can leave and return to your suite.

Had disgusting snack at the 'Buffet' on our floor with Svetlana who took us through our itinerary for the week in Moscow.

FIRST IMPRESSION OF HOTEL: it looks, feels and smells like a cross between a transport caff and our packaged hotel in Austria when we were skiing with the school • • •

M. • • • First sight of Russia from plane was of green fields and tall white tower blocks – the Just Like England refrain began. First Russian we saw was a burly lad in

24

charge of the exit chute thing. Airport was empty and dim
– v. keen on subdued lighting. We marched out first,
smiling and trying our Stratvys (hello) on every lackey –
no response. The passport control was v. le Carré –
youth in glass booth, big peaked hat, outstanding pimples.
When he directed us out with a pashalsta (please) and we
cooed spasseeba (thanks) – no response. About to go
through customs when Marina arrived – lovely calm,
gentle lady, good sense of humour. Ride to Moscow like
any other ride from airport in big cities – perhaps not so
much traffic, cars small and oldish. Our hotel is shabby-
grand with frowsty smell but an interesting feel to the
vestibule – party of priests going through – lots of
activity. Endless wait at desk with mountains of paperwork. We'd been booked into separate rooms. It was only
because I had a BM card, with my maiden name and
photo on, that we got together.

Svetlana now in charge. Her energy is formidable –
listening to her gives me a headache. And she bustles all
the time, all bright and lively – like a squirrel to Marina's
wonderful cow/doe-like presence. Laid into John Roberts
– how he's using the Writers Charter to his own ends,
etc. Took us to our room – endless corridors, then
double wooden doors opening into a veritable apartment
– 1 big sitting room with *piano* and tele and a sofa for
Flora to sleep on; I bedroom with 2 hard dwarf beds, a
pointless huge hall, bathroom and loo. All furnished/dec.
1930s style tho' also a feeling of attempted grandeur –
the chandelier, the polished wooden floors. Loo 'orrible
– black dusty pipes, leaking loo itself. View from our
room of a sort of courtyard – rather grand – big double-
locked windows opening onto it.

Met Svetlana in the buffet – oh my gawd – like the
worst kind of station buffet. She'd already ordered, to my
horror – ghastly sausages, stale white bread, what looked
like apricot jam, and a sort of macaroon. Cut up the

sausage and hid it in a napkin. Svetlana seemed so busy taking us through the itinerary that she didn't notice and wow was she eating well herself. Eventually she called attention to the 'jam' which we *must* have – it was red caviar, delish., even on stale white bread. The macaroons weren't bad either • • •

I didn't expect to be actually given money for our trip. You can't get roubles in England, so I'd just taken about £200 in English money, plus 100 dollars, left over from California, and my Visa card. But, in our room, Marina very solemnly handed over 216 roubles for our Moscow stay, plus 60 for the Black Sea hols. (One rouble equals roughly one pound.) I wondered which committee had arrived at that sum.

Marina went off in her car to her own apartment, which is apparently not far away, but Svetlana lives on the other side of Moscow. She said she was going to catch the Metro. We said we would walk with her, give us some exercise. Flora isn't usually keen on the word exercise, but I think she too fancied a look around our immediate neighbourhood.

We went through a little park where a bloke in an old suit and a red armband was lolling on a bench smoking and chatting. Svetlana said his armband meant he was a voluntary watchman, sort of local vigilante, keeping an eye on his little patch, making sure no one dropped litter, made a nuisance. He didn't seem to be doing much, but it was true that Moscow, from the few streets we'd seen so far, was incredibly tidy and litter-free.

Svetlana pointed out a few shop windows, all closed as it was now late and getting dark. Margaret and Flora looked at a few, and were obviously not very impressed. They seem to have nothing in them at all, just piles of dusty cans of suspicious-looking fish. Svetlana assured us that one particular shop did sell gifts and we would like it. We pressed our noses to the glass. All it had inside was a scruffy oriental-style carpet, hanging on a bare wall.

We walked back on our own from the Metro, assuring Svetlana we did know the way. Margaret and Flora have excellent senses of direction. I can get lost anywhere, even going to the lavatory in my own house. Svetlana had made a great thing about telling us we could walk freely round Moscow. On the way back, through the dark streets, we played spot the tail. If there was one, we didn't see it.

It did feel very safe, despite the dark and being in a completely strange town, walking amongst tall, high-rise housing blocks, the sort of area where you would walk rather carefully in London.

I did at last find a shop that was open, quite a large supermarket, and I said I wanted to go inside and explore. They moaned and said no, it's too late, we're all tired, leave it for tomorrow, let's get back to the hotel. I said it's sociological. I can't wait to investigate my first Russian shop. Hold on. Won't be a minute.

I was after only one thing. I'd already noticed that in the Ukraine Hotel there seemed to be no bar, at least I'd not seen one so far, and our bedroom fridge was totally bare. Inside the shop there were several vast open fridges, all with strange-looking tins, but most of the shelves were bare. There was one queue in a corner, but I couldn't work out what was being sold. Vegetables, I think. I eventually found a shelf full of bottles, but all of them seemed to contain fruit juice, or *soc* as they call it in Russia.

I rehearsed the words for beer and wine in my head, and excuse me please, can you help me, practised my smile, then approached several people, trotting out my prepared plea. Everyone stared right through me, as if I didn't exist.

Back in the hotel, Margaret said she agreed with Mr

Gorbachev. It was a good idea to cut down on drink and for the next few weeks, while we were in Russia, she was going to drink no alcohol. What a prig she can be at times.

I hadn't got the rules straight yet, or what precisely had happened to Russia, but according to Marina, one day in May 1985, people actually saw wine bottles disappearing off the tables, before their very eyes. That was the day the new regulations came in. Now it is an enormous battle to get a drink anywhere in Russia, except if you are very lucky and know where to queue and it's between two o'clock in the afternoon and seven o'clock. I know Russia has had problems with drunkenness for centuries, but it did seem a bit drastic.

I could feel a deep sulk coming on as I got into bed. That was quite a struggle, understanding the Russian form of duvet, wondering about the two starched sheets which looked like tablecloths, deciding that the solid rock of a pillow would have to go, and the scratchy blanket.

At least I had my five titchy bottles of British Airways wine, and one bottle of whisky. I'd given the other to Svetlana as a present, before the drink situation had fully dawned on me. Flora, did I give that visiting card to you? The one from the Ghana Ambassador to Moscow. I could be needing it . . .

CHAPTER THREE

Old Sights and Modern Scenes

We slept in next morning which was a surprise as the two single beds in our room had looked very lumpy and uncomfortable. It had been very quiet as our suite, number 628, was at the back of the hotel on the sixth floor. We then waited ages for the lift, giving up in the end and walked down some backstairs, which was what everyone else seemed to be doing. Going up was okay. Not down. Perhaps the up lifts shoot straight past the twenty-ninth floor, up into the heavens, and are never seen again.

We had decided to try breakfast in the posh restaurant downstairs, where we had caught sight of a funny-looking orchestra the night before. Hotel cards had to be produced to get in, which was rather pointless as the head waitress then waved her hands, indicating we were too late, pointing to the clock which showed a couple of minutes past ten. I put on my dumb look, poor foreign tourist, so she marched us through to demonstrate all the empty tables. It all looked a bit grim. Trays of cold spam and hard-boiled eggs and hunks of grey-looking bread.

Marina came for us at eleven o'clock to take us on our first sightseeing tour of Moscow. She had a taxi waiting outside, a beat-up-looking middle-range car, like an old Ford Cortina. They only have three basic cars in Russia – small, middle and large. Makes things very easy. Marina's was a small one, a Zhiguli (exported abroad as a Lada) of which she was very proud. Only 1 in 44 people in the Soviet Union has a car of his or her own. She explained it was really her mother's car which she had inherited. Middle size, like the Volga, is what taxi drivers use, or better-off professional people. The large size, big black brutes, are for Party people only. You can't buy them. I'd been led to believe we would see them speeding up the middle of every road, breaking the rules, taking the Bosses out to lunch, but I hadn't seen one so far.

Our taxi driver drove like a maniac, screeching round bends on two wheels. He didn't have his seat belt on, though it is compulsory, and just laughed when I put mine on. I couldn't get over how much traffic there was, but even more amazing was the space for the traffic. Moscow seems to have been flattened and then rebuilt, especially for drivers. There are massive ring roads and boulevards, right round the heart of the city, stretching for miles, and absolutely straight. Pedestrians take their lives in their hands if they try to cross, which they shouldn't do anyway as there are regular underpasses on the main roads. At one set of traffic lights, I did a quick count and worked out we were on a sixteen-lane highway – eight lanes of traffic, either side. It was as if a double-sized M6 had been put right in the middle of London, replacing Oxford Street. How on earth did they get away with it? I suppose it was Stalin's doing. He gets the blame for most things now regretted.

I was of course struck by the lack of advertising. No

commercial hoardings or posters anywhere. Such a relief on the eye, though there are often Communist-party slogans, stuck high on tops of roofs, telling about the triumphs of the recent 27th Party Congress. I asked Marina now and again what each slogan meant, pointing precisely to what I was yattering about. Like most locals, she doesn't see them any more. Part of the landscape.

The overall effect, of the huge housing blocks and the urban motorways, was boring and dull, rather than frightening or authoritarian. You can see such cityscapes in Paris, when you come in from the airport, or in London on the North Circular. There just happens, in Moscow, to be a hell of a lot of it.

It was, therefore, a big surprise to reach Red Square. Not just the vastness of it, about ten times the size of Trafalgar Square, but it was architecturally staggering, with so many grand buildings and monuments and spires and glittering roofs. Beside it, guarded by an enormous red wall, is the Kremlin, again much bigger than I had imagined, though I'm not quite sure what I had in mind. I thought perhaps the Kremlin might be one building, not realising till our Russian lessons that Kremlin in Russian means fort or citadel. I should have expected it to be more like a walled city, which is what it still is.

Red Square and the Kremlin have been the heart of Moscow since the first wooden Kremlin was built in 1156. On old maps, you can see how it was always surrounded by a system of concentric defences, reflected now in the horrible autobahns that go round and round the inner city. Coming in on these nasty modern roads you expect the centre to be a cement factory, or a hydro-electricity station, not an architectural masterpiece. The Poles ravaged Red Square in the seventeenth century, which is hard to believe today. Napoleon got there in 1812, and his army gutted three quarters of the city. The square still has a military feel, not just because we are used to seeing

31

Soviet processions there on TV, but the cobbled square, with the castle walls behind, does look like a parade ground, where an enormous army could easily assemble, ready to march on the world.

The taxi dropped us off near St Basil's Cathedral, the oldest building in the square, built in 1534. It was our first onion-domed Russian church, the sort you see in all the books and postcards, the typical Russian church, except that it was somehow over the top, a joke version, with about ten different domes and spires, all in mad designs, with pyramids and pineapple shapes, as well as the familiar onion blobs, and all of it in glorious technicolour, blues and reds, greens and yellows. It was as if a child had been let loose with a box of crystallised ginger and been told to pile on as many bits as possible.

It stands all on its own, an eccentric red lady, left over from some fancy dress parade, with traffic swirling all around. It's now a museum, not a church. At one time, there were scores of magnificent churches all over Moscow, but now almost all have gone. We decided not to explore inside. It was too nice a day and there was too much to see.

The Kremlin itself, so striking from afar, was slightly disappointing at first. We entered the walls and came to a massive modern building, all glass and concrete, which Marina told us proudly was the new Palace of Congress, a conference centre for Government meetings which can hold 6,000. But, once past that, everything inside the Kremlin was remarkable, especially the cathedrals and towers.

In several of the buildings we went into there was a lady sitting alone at a little desk with the word 'Consultant' in front of her. I went up to one, determined to find out what consultations she did, getting ready my few words of Russian, but at that moment she was very intently consulting her fingernails, staring at them, as if she was having a vision. I left her to it.

Near one of the cathedrals, we came across a group of Russian soldiers, all lined up like a football team for one of their number to take a snapshot. They had grouped themselves near an old canon, a Russian Mons Meg, their faces set in shy smiles, ready for the camera. I said to Margaret quick, get a photo of me standing beside them, but they all stood up by the time she had properly focused, their smiles forgotten, straightening their trousers, straightening their faces. I was left with the image, if not the photograph.

M. • • • Beautiful standing in the cobbled little squares looking round at all the dazzling gold domes and then inside the icons were magnificent – deep rich glowing dark colours almost shining. The smaller ones in particular were so vivid they looked painted yesterday. As designs they were curiously modern – many geometric – and included trees and hills and houses. Every inch of the interior walls was covered with faded frescoes in smudged, subtle colours that contrasted with the sharp icons. Same type of women on the gate each time – fat, bossy, humourless. Hunter winced as they cut/tore his tickets into shreds – can't get them for his scrapbook tho' Marina tried to salvage one • • •

F. • • • Went to the Kremlin which is in fact four or five buildings, well, cathedrals all in white with beautiful golden domes, very picturesque. Trailed in and out looking at the icons and other paintings that covered every wall and pillar as well as the ceiling of each church.

Mum appeared to admire them greatly, but pretty boring for *moi* • • •

We came back into Red Square which was full of tourist parties, all with leaders, carrying umbrellas or other means of identification. It had been fairly empty, first thing, when we'd started out at St Basil's, now all the charabancs had arrived and there were crowds everywhere. From their voices, the faces and the clothes, it was clear that almost everyone was from the various Soviet republics, as much strangers as we were, come from thousands of miles away, to gaze and to wonder, on a pilgrimage to a shrine they had only ever heard about. They were indeed worshippers as much as tourists. Moscow was known by Russians as the Holy City in the old days, and it still is today. It's the faith which brings them here, as well as the history and architecture, just as the faith takes people to Jerusalem or Rome. Instead of coming to pray by the Weeping Wall, or be blessed by the Pope at St Peter's, all good Russians come to genuflect before the embalmed body of Lenin.

The queue, dear God, the queue, at least two miles long, threading round the square, right under the Kremlin Wall, then on and on into the distance. They were all standing so patiently, but then Russians are born queuers. There were parties of soldiers and sailors, schoolchildren, young Communists with their sashes, as well as ordinary individuals, all looking so clean and spruce, as if going to church, all in their Sunday best. Marina said she could jump a bit of the queue for us, as we were Western tourists, allowed priority, but it would still mean a two-hour wait. When you do get in, you have to keep walking. With only a quick glance at the body, and it's all over in seconds.

Flora decided she would like an ice cream, so we

34

walked round the square towards some gardens, the Alexander Gardens. I'd sensed lots of people looking at Margaret and Flora, so different in their Western dresses and shoes. I'd even seen some nudging each other and pointing, after we had passed, all very subtly and shyly.

A group of Mongolian girls suddenly stopped in front of us, full on, and started jabbering away. Marina was a few steps behind at the time and I had no idea at first what they wanted. They took Margaret and Flora by the hands, all linked arms, and gave huge smiles while their boy-friends stood back on the pavement and snapped away. No one seemed to want my photograph. And I had on my best M&S trainers. The girls were from Tashkent, very friendly and outgoing, not like the native Moscow people we'd seen so far who had been very reserved, never smiling on the street, refusing to catch your eye.

We were still discussing the girls when we bumped into a bridal party. Then we saw others, getting out of black taxis, the brides working their way awkwardly in their high heels and bridal dresses along the crowded pave-ments, followed by their grooms and their attendants, just like any European wedding, but perhaps a bit more old-fashioned. The taxi drivers, sitting waiting for them, looked like taxi drivers anywhere, rather scruffy, rather bored, much more street-wise than the bridal parties, yet on the front of the cars several had hung bridal ribbons and corn dollies.

We followed one bridal party, to see where they were going, and watched them climb some low steps beside the red wall of the Kremlin, then lay their flowers on the tomb of the Russian unknown warrior. I could see the flame burning low down, from a vase in the ground. It was all very informal, with no one apparently organising them. Each party waited its turn to stand beside the flame, then they moved off a few yards, and had their photographs taken. It has become a tradition for newly-marrieds to

35

come to Red Square, straight from the register office, that's if they are good Communists. I noticed several people wearing red sashes, signifying local party leaders. But it had a religious feeling, rather than secular, a holy ritual, to put a blessing on their marriage.

We queued for ice-cream from an old woman standing behind an improvised stall, unpacking the blocks from brown cardboard boxes. Inside, the ice-cream was in cheap, grey paper, like wartime paper, with no attempt at packaging or display. There was only one sort, a plain chocolate roll, but it was delicious. Not long after we got ours, her supply ran out and she packed up her stall and disappeared. We had obviously been lucky to be there, just when she'd opened up for business.

We sat on a bench, eating our ice-creams, beside two youths doing a newspaper crossword together, and watched all the people going past, the bridal parties and the tourists. It could have been St James's Park in London, with all the gleaming spires beyond, except for the brides.

I remarked how well-dressed everyone was, though feeling a bit patronising for saying so, but Margaret said I was daft, and so started a long argument. She said I didn't know what I was talking about. I really meant 'well-dressed' in the sense of being clean and tidy, not necessarily fashionable. I did think they looked quite smart. Not perhaps Bond Street. More like Carlisle. I suppose the most obvious difference from London is the lack of variety. You don't get either punks or the extremes of high fashion, but on the other hand you don't get the scruffs, the tramps, the dirty, the dingy. They were all fresh and neat, if all very much the same.

There were lots of jeans around, mainly from Poland and East Germany. They are considered not as good as genuine Western jeans, but they looked fine to me. A crowd shot of the people in Red Square would look much like a crowd shot of tourists anywhere. I bet you wouldn't be able to tell which town they were in. Margaret said I was raving. All Russians look utterly *Russian* in all their clothes. Oh, well.

M. • • • Now we've seen more, it's possible to say the people are very old-fashionedly dressed rather than poorly. Women wear *frocks* with nipped waists and shortish skirts and high heels. Materials are garish patterns, poor colours. Old women wear kerchiefs on their heads and big cardigans. There *are* more vast women than thin.

The nicest sight today was that of brides walking round the square. The bridegrooms looked so shabby and seedy in ill-fitting suits and very embarrassed but the brides were sweet. They carried thin bouquets of lilies or gladioli or carnations still wrapped in cellophane.

Except for the Tashkent girls smiling, we still get no response and we arouse no curiosity. The whole place, for a capital, seems very countryfied, the pace slow. Absolutely no heavies anywhere – neither police nor soldiers. A great ordinariness about the people too – they strike one not so much as downtrodden as workaday, very working class. Haven't seen a single 'smart'-looking person. The almost total absence of hoardings and shop windows doesn't exactly make streets drab as a little lifeless. Must ask Marina why everything seems so *new* – I mean, Moscow wasn't bombed, was it? • • •

In the afternoon, we went to Moscow's Central Market, a range of large halls and outdoor stalls, selling a wide range of fruit and vegetables. There was one hall given over completely to cream cheeses while a whole row of outdoor stalls sold only strange-shaped yellow mushrooms. There was no sign of deprivation, which is what most Western people expect, believing there is never anything to buy in

37

Russia. It was as well-stocked an open-air market as I have seen anywhere in the world. Yet there were so few customers. Were they scared of radiation? Was it illegal to buy from stall-holders? Then I realised – the prices. They were astronomical. I was going to buy some plums for Margaret, as she does like them, till I found out they were £6 for one kilo. In the end I did let them have a bunch of weedy-looking carrots, Vitamin C for their morning breakfast. I'm not a hard man, though I could sense Flora was disappointed.

F. ● ● ● Went to market at about 3.00 pm which was rather like Portuguese markets – full of peasant stall-holders, mainly old women with amazing faces and headscarfs shaking around battered-looking vegetables – except there were hardly any customers. Dad went mad after announcing we wanted a water melon and making Marina ask the bloke how much and he nearly fainted after working out it was the equivalent of £16! Bloody 'ell, give me a London street market any day.

Back in our hotel I put the television on in the background. All that seems to be on is sport, nature programmes, and cartoons. What about old *East Enders*, eh? ● ● ●

While Flora rested in her room before the evening's excitement, doing her diary, so I hoped, and Margaret lay on her bed, reading a book, I went to explore the hotel. I wanted to get to the bottom of this drink business. I'd been unable all day to find beer or wine in any shops. We had seen one enormous queue, about half a mile long, while in the taxi, which was rumoured to have been for vodka. When the new law came in, nine-tenths of the wine places closed at once. Hence the queues, should one shop chance to open.

It must have deprived hundreds of thousands of people of their jobs, in the vineyards, the distribution trade, the bars, the wine shops, yet I presume the real alcoholics will always be prepared to queue.

You might of course queue for three hours, and get only one bottle, as it's always rationed, or none at all, if they've run out, or if the queue wasn't for drink after all. Russians join any queue they see, always carrying their little 'perhaps' string bag with them, just in case, then they find out afterwards what the queue is for.

There was once a bloke in a vodka queue who suddenly went mad, having stood for three hours, getting nowhere. He pulled out a knife and said that's it, I've had enough, I'm going to the Kremlin to get Gorbachev. He stormed off, and the queue moved up one place. He returned about an hour later and people asked him what had happened, why hadn't he knifed Gorbachev, as he'd vowed. 'I wanted to,' he said. 'But the queue at the Kremlin was longer than here.' That's a modern classic amongst Russian jokes. I was told it four times.

I was looking for the 'Beriozka', or little silver birch tree, which is the name for the special shop for Western tourists only. I eventually found one in our hotel, on the first floor. It had been closed every time I'd gone past it so far, and I thought anyway it was purely for souvenirs. In a Beriozka you can only spend Western currency which no Russian can ever get hold of, not roubles. It was well-stocked, and very reasonable, with whisky about £6 a bottle, cheaper than England. I bought two bottles of wine, four beers and, as an afterthought, some Cokes for Flora, then I went triumphantly back to our room.

Flora refused the Coke, saying she had given it up. Margaret declined everything. She'd already told me she was off alcohol. Didn't I listen? It was pathetic the way I

39

put so much enthusiasm into looking for drink.

I lay on my bed, swigging beer from the can, oh, the luxury of it all. I must have gone all of twenty-four hours without a drink. It felt like being in the army, though I've never actually been in the army. Margaret was on her bed, still reading away, so I got out the Colin Thubron and spent the next hour with him and his dissidents, till it was time to get dressed, poshed up, ready to go out on the town.

Once again, we got a mad taxi driver who drove like the clappers, out into the suburbs, about ten miles from the centre, in amongst some very modern high-rise blocks, near the Izmailov Park. The blocks had been built for the Moscow Olympics, part of the Olympic village, and were now hotels. We came to one marked Hotel B, but couldn't find how to get in. Marina had never been before. Svetlana had apparently been ringing round Moscow to find a disco that would be on this evening.

Inside, it was much more presentable. A large ballroom on the ground floor had been laid out with little tables and chairs, with a small stage at one end for the disco music. We got a table at the front, as we appeared to be the first ones in, then it slowly filled up. There was a bouncer on the door, about six foot six tall, watching people as they came in, though everyone was in their best clothes and looked terribly respectable. It even struck me that they were smart and contemporary, but I didn't want to start arguing with Margaret again. The girls especially looked like girls in a disco anywhere. Though, what do I know about discos?

Two very flash-looking disc jockeys, one wearing a Nike top, were setting up their amps and turntables, testing their loudspeakers. A Russian of about thirty came over and very hesitatingly sat down beside us and in halting

English talked about all the English pop groups he loved. He'd guessed we were English, having overheard us talking. As we chatted, the younger of the DJs came over and started speaking Russian to us. It was becoming rather confusing. Our new friend laughed, explaining later that the DJ had assumed we were from the Moscow Soviet (the local government body in Moscow) and he was asking if there were any tunes he should *not* play.

The first record they played was 'Girl', the old Beatles number, from the album 'Rubber Soul'. It was from the original album, not a cover job. They played records for about the first hour, half of them English or American, half Russian, the DJ in the Nike introducing each number in what sounded like a mid-Atlantic Russian accent.

Nobody danced during this first hour, just listened and ate supper. Entrance to the disco was one rouble, but for four roubles more you got the set meal, served at your table. It consisted of two rolls, hard and tasteless on the outside, but inside they had been stuffed with smoked salmon. Then there were hard-boiled eggs, stuffed with black caviar, the inevitable macaroon cakes, plus sweets and coffee. It was served rather nicely by waitresses and waiters, yet somehow it was unappetising, despite the salmon and caviar. Even in Russian shops, such things are not cheap. Flora and Margaret declined their food. I ate my own, plus everyone's fillings. The coffee was Turkish, thick and black and delicious.

After supper, the floor show began, starting with a group of dancers, boys and girls, who demonstrated different sorts of dancing styles, all to pop records, doing little scenes, like a pop ballet. There was a conjuror who I thought was very good. He took people from the audience and pulled money out of their ears and pockets and from inside their shirts. I was hoping to be picked, but he didn't reach us.

One of his tricks was to take a pack of cards and make

41

shapes out of them. He finished by throwing the whole pack in the air, making the cards form a question mark. He then laid the pack of cards across his chest, as if it were a sash, the sort young Communist Party officials wore. Finally he turned the pack into the shape of a large screw, and pretended to screw it into his ear, as if indicating someone was mad. There was loud laughter and applause. It seemed to me this particular sequence of tricks was symbolic – was he saying that joining the Communist Party was madness? I asked Margaret and Flora if they had noticed anything, but they couldn't even remember the trick. Neither could Marina. They thought I was going a bit potty. Too many cheap thrillers. Or perhaps it was the fault of the Colin Thubron. In his book, based on a car trip through Russia, all he ever seems to meet are cynical or drunken dissidents, all hating the state, all dying to get out. He was of course staying in scruffy camp sites. We were in a modern hotel, amongst nice people. Surely there would be no subversive elements here.

I looked around at all the young people enjoying themselves. Most were aged about twenty, laughing and talking, groups of girls together, and boys together, as well as couples, with perhaps parties from the same office. It was noisy, with lots of yells and shouts, but there were no rowdies.

I saw a bloke coming back to his table with lots of bottles, so I jumped up at once and made for a bar in the far corner where there were a lot of people milling around. What a disappointment. It was boring old Russian juice, the sweet brown water they drink all the time, though some of the smaller bottles looked interesting, till I very slowly translated what the labels said. It was Fanta and Pepsi, in Russian. I told Flora, but she refused them as well.

The highlight of the evening was a group of three boys,

dressed in street clothes, jeans and Adidas track suit tops, who suddenly bounded into the middle of the dance floor. At once the whole audience surged forward, leaving their tables, as if they were expecting these boys. The earlier dancers had been very arty, actorish and stagey, but these three boys did look as if they had come straight from Camden Town High Street. They started doing break dancing, something I've never seen before in the flesh.

They got tremendous applause when they finished. It had been very exciting. Everybody then started dancing, the usual sort of Western dancing, a few feet apart, moving the top half of your body in that boring half-witted way. Give me Sixties jiving any time. Margaret of course never dances. I didn't bother asking her. Marina graciously agreed, so I did have a go. Just for England. Got to fly the flag.

We all sat down again and I thought what a good time everyone is having, 200 or so young people, well-behaved, dancing and listening to the sort of pop music the whole world is currently dancing and listening to. We could be with modern youth anywhere, Paris, New York or London, except for two things. Not a drink had passed anyone's lips. Not a single joint had been handed round. Who needs artificial stimulation?

The DJ came over to our table again, said something to Marina, who then asked if I'd mind going on the stage and being presented. She had apparently told him I was the author of the Beatles biography. Naturally, I accepted the invitation. She came up with me and translated as I spoke for about ten minutes, chuntering on about the Beatles.

Two youths approached me afterwards and said they had read my book some years previously, underground copies, translated into Russian, which had been passed from hand to hand. That was news to me. I'd already had it confirmed from Marina that the Beatles are heroes in Russia, especially John Lennon. She too had read my book, but an English copy, brought in by a friend. A small world, my masters.

7.00 pm Disco!

F. • • • It was in a huge room full of tables and chairs with an old-fashioned dance floor with the classic silver-mirrored ball turning on the ceiling giving out spots of coloured light that spin on the walls just to classify it as a 'disco'. Two 'Tony Blackburn'-type DJ's spinning at least 7 yr old bubble gum music on spotlighted record players. Also had performing dancers, pathetic troop of 'disco dancers' but funny, and also 3 amazing . . . breakdancers (?!) Pretty good, considering. Amazing to think hip-hop has got to the USSR. Crowd gathered round and applauded excitedly. Breakdance now appears ultra trendy. I think some of them have been watching too much of *Fame*, judging by the outfits and practising their 'COOL, HARD' looks in the mirror and all the dancers wearing 'HARVARD UNIV.' sweatshirts or American Football tops.

Dad made a speech (pass the sick bag) in front of completely confused Muscovites who managed to clap at his boasting about how – : '. . . and I lived with the Beatles for 18 months . . .' etc. to dad's satisfaction. What a happy little boy! • • •

M. • • • Hunt certainly enjoyed it. My gawd – he loved it – rushed with M. to the microphone, great applause, and I cringed . . . He made a v. boring speech about his book, translated by M. piece by piece, missing any opportunity to give them some personal connection with Paul. I thought he could've said how amused and thrilled the Beatles would be to know their records are still played in Moscow or something. But he was pleased with himself

44

and the audience v. good natured. The lights went out promptly at 11. No messing. Taxi home – another Hard Man who drove furiously. Will we ever get even a half-gracious, friendly driver?

We passed the KGB building on the way home, 2 Dzerzhinsky Square, which Hunt worked out from one of his guide books. Lovely building. Easy to forget it exists, when everything and everyone seem so harmless so open and happy and modern • • •

CHAPTER FOUR

A Religious Experience and a Sociological Supper

The next day was Sunday so what better than a ride out into the country, perhaps take in a church. The immediate countryside around Moscow is flat and rather ordinary, nothing at all exciting, though the woods were pleasant enough and it was interesting when we started seeing dachas, the little wooden country cottages, used by Moscow's Hampstead types for their weekend breaks.

We were heading for Zagorsk, about forty miles north-east of Moscow. It was another mad driver, tearing down the freeways at ridiculous speeds. He was smoking, despite a notice in his own car saying 'No Smoking', and of course he had no seat belt on. I don't know why I ever thought Russians were law-abiding.

When I moaned, through Marina, that perhaps he could go a little more slowly, so we could enjoy the lovely views of the dachas and give my stomach a chance, he then dropped to a sullen 20 mph crawl. He kept this up for ages, till we all begged for mercy, and he then proceeded at a more acceptable speed.

For the last 500 years Zagorsk has been the religious capital of Russia, their Canterbury Cathedral and home of the Patriarch of the Russian Orthodox Church. It's a walled town, like the Kremlin, and I expected it to be simply a museum village, like the Kremlin, with secularised tourist sites. After all, it's over sixty years since the Bolsheviks started religious persecution, though during the last war there was a slight change in attitude when it was realised that the Church could be used in the fight against the Nazis. The Church is now technically not illegal, but it is actively discouraged, and the Party keeps up an intense atheistic propaganda. There were 54,000 churches in Tsarist days. Now there are only 7,500.

We parked outside the white walls of the old town and set off to explore the immaculate cathedrals and churches, little gardens and squares. When the Russian film industry needs a genuine period setting, they often use Zagorsk. We wandered from church to church, gazing up at the gleaming domes, mingling with all the other tourists, but when I tried to get into the biggest church, we couldn't. It was full. There was a service going on and I could see the candles through a crack in a doorway, the incense burning and voices chanting. The crowds outside in the squares were like us, tourists come to gape, but inside the churches were full of real worshippers. And it wasn't just oldies, or peasant women. I could see lots of young men and women and families, sitting and praying inside. I tried a side-door but there were worshippers there as well, obediently standing outside, unable to get in, but following the service.

We got into a smaller chapel, observing a notice not to take photographs, where hordes of women were queuing up to kiss various icons and relics, bending down on the floor to reach them, pushing and shoving each other,

47

desperately rubbing their hands all over the objects and paintings. There was a tremendous atmosphere of religious fervour. Fanaticism almost. Perhaps even panic.

I went back to the main cathedral and queued up again and this time I managed to push through a slight gap and get into the entrance hall. It was very crowded and rather sweaty with all the bodies. One of the reasons for the crush was the presence of a row of old peasant women, stationed against one wall, holding out their hands for money.

'Why are you begging?' said a rather bossy Russian lady in front of me. 'You get a pension, don't you?'

The beggar woman's answer was rather gruff and I didn't quite catch it, so I asked Marina who had come in behind me. 'None of your business.' That's what Marina translated it as. I suspect it was more like the Russian equivalent of 'piss off, bitch'.

Outside in the gardens, I tried to photograph a few of the priests, but they shied away when they saw my camera. So I photographed the Boris Godunov family grave, never realising he was real, not just an operatic creation. I saw a few more priests, so I made Margaret go and stand near them so I could pretend I was really taking her. Many of them were young and handsome. There is a seminary as part of the complex, which now has a waiting list.

Religion is obviously alive and reasonably well in Russia today, part of the resurgence of interest by Russians in their own history. The Russian Orthodox Church is of course Russian, part of the country's culture, so it would be difficult to kill it off, and silly to ignore it, but there does seem to be a genuine desire for spiritual comfort, despite the efforts of the Communist Party. It will be the millennial celebrations of the Russian Orthodox Church in 1988 – and it's said the Pope himself might turn up. A Polish Pope, going to Communist Russia, to celebrate Christianity.

F. • • • Spent what seemed like a v. long time looking at Zagorsk's so-called famed architectural monuments, the white stone Trinity Cathedral with enormous gold domes and other coloured carved-out buildings in a very twee square that looked like something out of a fairy tale. Millions of bent-over old women huddled and pushed in and out with their burning candles and cups for a sup of the ole' holy water. (Grandma would have blended in well.) With the mixed smell of wax and old women, it soon became very claustrophobic • • •

Marina, as a treat, said she would take us to a very nice restaurant, the Russian Fairy Tale, on the main road back towards Moscow, so we got all excited, but when we got there it was closed. There were some lads outside, flogging kebabs from a rough barbecue, throwing around huge slabs of dodgy meat, but even I wasn't willing to try them. M and F, being veggies, felt sick at the very sight.

So we drove on, towards Moscow, looking out for any likely places. We saw nothing. I had already grown resigned to the fact that you don't get bars or cafés in Moscow, the sort that sell real coffee or real drinks, but now I realised how few eating places there were. Perhaps the Russians all eat and booze at home.

Marina vaguely remembered being told about a Georgian restaurant, so she stopped and asked a passer-by. We then set off on a trail into the interior, asking all the time, till we came to a railway line, where the taxi had to stop as there was no crossing. We walked over it, something we would never do on a main line in England, and came to a sort of shanty town, with unmade roads and piles of rubble. We found the restaurant at last, dusty on the outside, with windows that had never been washed, but inside it was quite smart and rather busy. It had taken us so long that it was now well after two o'clock, so I thought goody, we might get wine, then I thought no chance, not out here, well off the tourist track.

All around there were hefty Russians throwing back the vodkas. Any wine? No, nor any beer. Just vodka, brandy or champagne. I quite fancied Russian champagne, just to try it, purely as an experiment, but no one else would have any and it only came by the bottle. Curses. I hate vodka and brandy so I had to have the dreaded juice which was already on the table. It was awful, and so was the meal, though I can't remember what it was.

F. • • • Had lunch in primitive Georgian-style café which consisted of cold beans, spiced beetroot, tomatoes and bread and no bloody alcohol to dad's horror. We were all presented with pomegranate flavoured water. (The sight of dad's face.)

Hunt was soon cheered up a little by finding a bookshop nearby and got all excited by buying Russian postcards, maps and posters, but poor Marina had trouble in translating what he wanted • • •

We had our first dinner party that night, our first visit to the home of a real Russian. Svetlana had fixed it up, one of three arranged for the week, and she came to our hotel to pick us up and take us there. I wondered how she had leaned on these people, what connection there was, what favours they owed. Perhaps they all jumped, out of the kindness of their hearts, competing to have two unknown English writers and their teenage daughter for dinner. Catch us knocking ourselves out for complete strangers in London.

Svetlana said we were going to an area of Moscow where lots of writers lived, but it was hard to believe. It looked just as crummy as any other housing blocks we had seen. Everyone is supposedly equal, as far as accommodation is concerned, but I had expected that eminent writers, and in this case a Professor, would have wangled a few extra facilities. His block looked just like the one in King's Cross where Caitlin, our older daughter, once squatted. The entrance hall was squalid and scruffy and Svetlana ushered us into a rickety old lift which didn't look as if it would get off the ground. As we went up, I could see that all the communal bits of the block, on each floor, were equally ill-kempt.

Inside the flat was better than outside, but it was in no sense luxurious and far from spacious. All he had were two small rooms – a bedroom and a living room – plus a pokey bathroom, more like a lobby than a bathroom, and a small cubicle of a kitchen. He also had a small balcony which he proudly took me on to. It was about three feet wide, just a concrete slab, but he'd rigged up a light and little desk and often worked there in the evenings, if it was warm.

All we'd known beforehand was that he was called Oleg Feofanov and that he was a Professor at some Sociology Institute and had written a few books. We don't have much in common with sociologists, and even in England it's hard to understand what they're on about. He turned out to be very entertaining, quick and witty, about my age I guessed, with brilliant English and an enormous breadth of interests.

His living room was dominated by a massive sound system, stereos and loudspeakers everywhere, and racks of tapes on every wall. Svetlana said he had the biggest collection of records of anyone she knew in Moscow. He'd apparently written three books on Russian rock and roll. You what? I didn't know you could write one page on it, never mind three books. He brought them out, and they were not very big, little more than booklets, rather academic-looking, but they were indubitably on rock and roll, and written in Russian. I recognised quite a few of the pictures, including J. Lennon.

He'd papered the walls of his little hall with American cigarette packets. An amusing little collection, I said. I have several similar potty collecting hobbies, such as postcards and old railway bonds, and I always enjoy looking at other people's passions. But this was a serious collection. He'd written a study of American mass advertising and used these cigarette packets, and their images, as an example of something or other.

I admired all his plants, which had been hung in every available space to brighten up the living room, and also an aquarium. He said he had three in all. He took me into his little kitchen, which was dominated by two massive aquaria. His startled wife tried to hide herself in a corner. She was slaving over a hot stove. She spoke no English and hardly appeared all evening.

I noticed a photograph of Oleg himself as a young man, very dashing and handsome, standing beside a huge American sports car. He said this was in Canada. At one time he'd been the press attaché at the Soviet Embassy there. It was his own car, bought by himself, not an Embassy one. He wished he had it now.

There was an air of genteel student poverty about the flat, apart from his impressive stereo equipment and books. The furniture was odd and didn't match and it had obviously been a struggle to decide how we should all be seated. A low card table had been set out in front of a hard-looking couch, with unmatching chairs at either side. It was laid for six, with an oddment of plates and cutlery.

Svetlana's seventy-year-old mother was already there, Katerina. We'd heard about her, and been told she is a distinguished writer and translator, a power in the Writers' Union. Svetlana is simply an official, not a writer herself.

M. • • • Katerina was wonderful. Small, bird-like, dynamic, brilliant rattling English much more idiomatic and easier to follow than Svet's. She *did* talk all the time but it was entertaining – great stories of falling in love with Andropov and he with her and of her start on the factory floor at a loom and gradual rise thro' getting elected to some post in the Party. She had a good sense of humour too, as well as being outrageously blunt. She complained about Oleg smoking his pipe, even tho' it was his flat, as I pointed out, only to be told 'and that's his balcony too'. Poor Oleg went out to stand on this scrap of a balcony.

The meal was delicious: small pieces of fish crisply fried in a spicy batter; a salad of tiny bits of fruit, nuts, chicken in a mayonnaise; a big platter of toms, cucumbers, lettuce, 'riga' (fresh aniseed?) and other greenery; roast chicken pieces – and then the pièce de résistance, the Cabbage Pie, oh my, what a sight – great golden oblong cut into squares with melting cabbage plus egg plus peas inside a golden pastry/sponge – yes, it sounds revolting but it was a true taste thrill. We ate far too much. There was booze too – Oleg was in despair that I wouldn't drink (out of respect for Gorbachev of course) but H obliged by consuming a whole bottle of white wine and a titchy bit of vodka. To finish there was delicately flavoured orange mousse like ice-cream and chocolates. I felt overwhelmed at such kindness when we don't know them and have no connection with them and he isn't even a writer • • •

I concentrated on talking to Oleg. In such a small room, having two noisy conversations going at the same time, I worried about Flora becoming bored or fed up, but then I thought hard cheese. A real Russian dinner party. What an experience. She can have all her fun on the Black Sea next week.

I told Oleg about going to Zagorsk and how amazed I

was at the obvious strength of Christianity in Russia, far greater than I had expected. He said the Government was still officially against religion, in the sense that they did not encourage it, but what could they do?

'Religion is growing because people think what have I lived for, what's the point, and they can't think of one, so they turn to religion. Ideology is not enough.'

He said he was an atheist, and he personally couldn't see any attraction, but as a Professor of Sociology he found the subject fascinating.

I took him up on the point about ideology not being enough. Was Communism therefore failing? He smiled at this. The problem was that exhorting people to work harder, which was what the Party had done for decades, in slogans and propaganda posters, was not working as well. 'Encouraging people to work for the good of the country is not enough. You must *interest* them. That's what we've now got to do.'

I asked if the Government was worried about this growth in religion, but he shrugged. 'The Government has got other things to worry about, such as the economy. That's first. Then they can worry about religion.'

Surely they must be concerned about all the *young* people? At Zagorsk, in the churches, it had been mainly old biddies, but there had been a surprising number of young men and women, and a great many young, handsome, priests.

Oh, the young priests, he said, with a leer. They just go into religion for the women.

But he admitted the Government was slightly worried about one aspect. It is becoming more and more common for Party members to have their children baptised in the Church. Covering themselves both ways? 'Probably, but what they also say is "We're doing it for the grandparents".'

After we'd finished eating and drinking, Oleg played us some tapes. He started with some Russian popular music, vaguely rock and roll, but more folksy. They all listened, even Katerina for once, when he put on something by a Russian singer who had recently died rather suddenly, a tape Oleg had recorded himself. Then there was some stuff from a dissident Russian, now in Paris.

When he's not listening to music, Oleg has on the BBC World Service. All news is biased, he said. Someone has to choose what to broadcast, so it's always someone's opinion, but on the whole he believed what the BBC said. He turned on his radio, adjusted a very long aerial, but there was just a lot of noise and interference. 'I think the Russians are jamming it,' he said, smiling. He tried a few more stations, then gave up. At this time of night, he said, only the Voice of Israel seems to get through.

He listens now and again to the Voice of America. 'But that's aimed at Russian Jews. I think 90% of their output is aimed at Jews, so it gets a bit boring.'

Katerina interrupted to tell a joke. There was this Russian who goes to the authorities because he wishes to emigrate. 'But why do you want to emigrate?' he's asked. 'You've got a good job, a big flat, a dacha, two cars, why do you want to go? Are you Jewish?' 'Yes,' says the man. 'I want to stay. It's my family who want to leave . . .'

She then went on to tell a Gorbachev joke, one he'd made at his own expense in a recent speech. Since the alcohol bans, he knew that people were no longer calling him General Secretary but Mineral Secretary. It's a joke that tells better in Russian, as the Russian words 'General'ny' and 'Mineral'ny' sound very similar. Ho ho.

Oleg then said he would play us something really interesting, which would amuse us, a record he had picked up during his years in North America. He put it on, sat back and smiled, watching our faces.

A sexy American voice started talking, in a very phoney posh English accent, while smoochy music played in the background. 'Oooh, do it again, darling. That was wonderful. Hmm. Darling. Please, please, please . . .'

The male voice started talking this time in a phoney Russian accent, with lots of sighs and heavy breathing. 'Oh, zat was vunderfool, my darlink. Pleez do eet, Chreesteen . . .'

Oleg waited for the penny to drop, till we eventually realised it was supposed to be Christine Keeler, a joke American record, put out at the time of the Profumo scandal. I'd never heard of it before.

Oh, what good fun it was in London in the Sixties, with a new revelation every day at one time, to entertain the nation. They don't make scandals like that any more. Oleg and I both agreed we were Sixties people.

He then went off and produced from a drawer a copy of a 1964 *Sunday Times*. The front page story was about Roy Thomson, then the owner of the *ST*, who went to Moscow to try to see Philby. There was a photograph of Thomson on the front. Yes, quite interesting. But so what? Oleg then drew my attention to the credit line on the photograph – Oleg Feofanov. How incredible. How had he come to take it? Well, he'd been working at the time for the Novosty news agency in Moscow, and had covered the story. His photograph had ended up in the *ST*. He'd even got paid. He's always been a keen photographer and has whole albums of mini-skirted girls in Hyde Park, taken in London in the Sixties.

I took the faded newspaper, and slowly turned over every page, and there in the Atticus column was what I was looking for – the name of yours truly. I explained I worked on the *ST* during the Sixties, doing the Atticus column. It was his turn to be amazed. Twenty-two years ago, we had our names in the same edition of the very same newspaper. Yet it's taken us all this time to meet. Yes, I will have another vodka. But just a small one, Oleg old chap.

As I left, I asked him what happened to Major Ivanov,

or was he a Colonel, the Russian Embassy military attaché involved in the Profumo affair, the one who had in effect brought down the British Government. He must have been fêted when he got home, I said, not just having got all the secrets, from the mistress of the War Minister, but stirring up a major scandal, then sneaking off before he ever got caught.

'Yes, he did come back to Moscow,' said Oleg. 'Then he had a heart attack and died. He was aged forty-two.'

What a bit of news, something I'd never heard before. On the way down the stairs, I tried to explain the significance of this bit of gossip to Flora, but she'd never heard of Christine Keeler, or Profumo, and she was rather exhausted by now, after three hours of what I thought had been a very good but rather noisy dinner party.

F. • • • The best thing was the cabbage pie. It was baked by his wife as a pudding (. . . yukky idea) but was warm and delicious. When asked how to make such a delicacy, he replied, 'oh, it's easy, just stick zee wife in zee kitchen for a couple of hours.'

Svetlana and her mother, (Katerina who writes poetry and puts together books of selected poems) were there. Katerina talked in jumbled English the entire time and butted in every conversation not directed to her, but was funny and amazing for a seventy-year-old young gal.

M + H enjoyed it greatly, but I was deadly bored all evening • • •

As we left Oleg's flat, trying to find a taxi, Katerina demonstrated jogging to us. She goes out every morning, she and her dog, in her track suit and trainers. People shout comments at her, but she doesn't care.

We couldn't get a taxi so she insisted we walk with her

to her flat and have some coffee. Svetlana didn't seem keen, but her mother frogmarched us along the street. Her block looked similar to Oleg's, perhaps in slightly better condition, but inside it was certainly an improvement. She had three rooms, kitchen and bathroom, all light and spacious. It seemed a lot, for just one old woman. How had she managed it?

She has a live-in man, she said, so that qualified her for one extra room. No, it wasn't her husband. He was a sort of house husband, so she explained. She writes, while he cleans the flat and cooks. There was no sign of him, but when we went into the bathroom, where there was a pile of medicines on a cabinet, she made it clear they were his, not hers. 'He's just a worker, not an artist. But, when we go to Latvia, everyone knows him. He used to be a big basketball star in Latvia.'

As for the third room, she qualified for that as a writer. She had helped to force through a rule whereby members of the Soviet Writers' Union qualify for an extra twenty metres of space. The theory being that they work from home.

She took us into her own room and showed us all her books. She's written thirty-five in all, translated into various Russian languages and editions. 'I have written too much, I think,' she said, looking down the shelves, as if she was referring to another person.

Before Svetlana finally got us away, she presented each of us with an apricot. 'Very good for the heart.'

We got the Metro home, as we failed completely to find a taxi, which was a great experience, even better than I had expected. I hadn't realised that every station is different, each trying to out-do the others in grandiose architecture, marble pillars and halls, massive chandeliers, sculptures and mosaics, lamps and ornate rails. As for the trains themselves, they were about the same size as in London, but very clean. It was like getting on an ordinary Tube train, only to find it was running through the National Gallery, Harrods' Food Hall, finishing inside Versailles.

Over 12 million people a day use Moscow's 123 stations and 200 kilometres of track. The lay-out, when you buy a Metro map, is not too different from London's, with nine different lines radiating from the middle, and a circle line going round.

They're extremely proud of it, boasting about the engineering wonders that had to be performed, the famous architects who won prizes to build each station. I'd bought a Russian guide book to Moscow, printed in English, which gives a little history, how it was built in 1935. It had been thought of before the Revolution, but never begun, the plans being rejected in 1902 because 'the tunnel will pass in places only a few feet beneath churches, the peace and quiet of these sacred places will be disturbed'. The message was clear. Hurrah for Soviet initiative.

We changed trains at Mayakovskaya Station, named in honour of the famous Russian poet. Many of the stations are called after writers and artists. There was a large statue of him at the end of the platform and someone had placed two fresh roses at his marble feet. Wouldn't it be nice if London tube stations were called Shakespeare Station, or Dickens Station, and decorated accordingly, instead of boring old Tufnell Park or Cockfosters?

The next Metro train we got on must have come directly from the outer suburbs. It was full of families carrying large baskets of fruit, masses of flowers, potatoes, raspberries, plus carrier bags and rucksacks full of weekend clothes and possessions. I could even smell some freshly-baked pies and cakes. Two women had them on their knees, carrying them carefully in straw baskets under gingham cloths, like young schoolgirls coming home from their first Domestic Science lessons. The smells and sights were instantly so rural, yet we were in the heart of underground Moscow. They had all been to their dachas for the weekend, so Svetlana explained. But they looked such ordinary working people. Why not? said Svetlana. Anyone in Russia can have a dacha.

I'd assumed such things were for top Party bosses, or successful artists, but she said that small, wooden dachas were quite cheap to buy. And you could *buy* them, own them yourself. There is now a widespread back-to-the-country fashion in Moscow, folks desperate for the Good Life, to have their own little rural hideaway, grow a few vegetables, return to nature.

Understandable, really, when you see the ugly, high-rise, concrete blocks in which they live their work-a-day lives. I suppose it's also part of that same pattern, which happens to people as they grow up, grow on, they start harking back to nature, just as they hark back to their history, and to their religion.

CHAPTER FIVE

Culture and Circus

I felt rotten in the night, with the most awful pains in my stomach. I blamed it on that cabbage pie. Or it could have been the vodka, combined with the bottle of wine. I took a couple of anti-acid tablets, and then another two. I got them in London about a year ago, convinced I was getting an ulcer, but they'd gone soggy in the meantime. I took six in the end before the pain subsided, then just when I was getting back to sleep, the bloody lavatory started. The system was prehistoric and I'd warned M and F on no account to pull the chain more times than necessary. The whole suite was soon shaking with the noise.

I got up and fixed it and eventually went to sleep. When I awoke, M and F were already up, sitting having their breakfast, a cup of cold water and some dry biscuits.

This is ridiculous, I said, going to the fridge and throwing it open. I'm not having dry biscuits and water. I searched all the shelves, just in case, and found some of the weedy carrots. 'Don't touch those,' shouted Margaret. 'They're counted.'

I'm going to the Buffet, trying to remember whether the Russians pronounce it 'Boo-feet-et' or 'Buff-yet'. It's one of the many Western words taken by the Russians, but they say it their own way. I took with me our bedroom teapot and a tea-bag, stolen from our secret supply of tea-bags, part of the clutch of presents to give to poor Russians. So far we'd not given away anything. I don't think those Taxi Heavies would appreciate postcards of our dear Queen and all Marina seemed interested in was British fashion magazines and British novels, and we hadn't brought nearly enough of them.

There was a huge queue in the Buffet, African students, Mongolian-looking women, Central Asian tourists, Russian businessmen, all waiting patiently. I only wanted some hot water poured into my teapot. So I went to the head of the queue, trying to catch the eye of the lady slopping out the dodgy-looking frankfurters and hunks of hard bread. She was very hefty and looked like Mrs Khrushchev.

I mumbled the Russian for hot water, please, and pointed to my teapot. She ignored me at first. Mrs Khrushchevs the world over know how to put queue-jumpers in their place. Then I asked again. She shouted some Russian at me and made various fierce gestures.

I looked down the queue for help, but of course there were no Brits. I never met one English-speaking tourist in the whole of Moscow. They were mostly from different parts of the Soviet Union, so I imagined, speaking their own language, plus Russian. I dragged myself to the end of the queue and stood in line like a good boy. I couldn't go back to our bedroom without a hot drink. They'd just scoff and mock, I know their sort.

Mrs Khrushchev was suddenly standing beside me, pushing me in the ribs, trying to steer me somewhere. Oh no, what have I done now? I should not have been horrible in my head about Russian public food. It's probably a crime against the State. I'd be on bread and water for weeks. Again.

I slowly realised that she was pointing me towards a

sliding door into the kitchen, telling me to go in. Which I did. There was a huge cauldron with a tap beneath, so I helped myself to hot water. Mrs Khrushchev gave me a big smile when I'd managed. Had I made a friend?

I went back along the corridor, feeling very chuffed. A whole pot of tea, all for me, what good times I'm going to have. I'm certainly not letting that selfish lot in the bedroom have any. They can fight their own wars.

What about milk? I stopped to think. I can do without sugar in tea, oh, I gave that up years ago, but I do like a spot of milk. Perhaps my new friend Mrs K would oblige.

I went to the top of the queue again, pushing my luck, I know, and asked for *moloko*. That's one of the words I had learned during our Russian lessons in London. Or did it mean ice-cream? I rolled it round my mouth, trying various pronounciations, permutating the syllables, hoping one of them would click. No luck. Mrs K did not look so friendly.

'Moo,' I said. 'Moo, moo.'

All very childish, but how else could I make it clear that I wanted milk. If, of course, Russian cows do go moo, otherwise they would be more confused. (Russian cockerels do *not* say Cock-a-Doodle-Doo. This is a fact. Ask any Russian. They go Ko Ka Roo Doo. See, I had learned something new.)

The whole queue started laughing, so wherever they came from, cows do go 'Moo, moo'. But I think some of them were laughing because they thought I was mocking the fierce Mrs Khrushchev, making rude noises at her, which honestly I wasn't. I wouldn't do that. I think she also suspected I was being cheeky, but she did eventually give me some milk.

Success at last. Won't those girls be jealous in the bedroom. Not a bad place, Russia, once you know how to work the system.

The first event of a very busy day was a visit to an Exhibition, the so-called V.D.N.Kh., which in Russian stands for the Exhibition of Economic Achievement. Margaret and Flora were not looking forward to this, but I was quite interested. It turned out to be another small town in itself, covering over 500 acres, with around eighty large pavilions, landscaped parks and gardens and a three-mile circular road with a miniature train from which you can see the whole complex in comfort. The Russians are mad about size. Big is beautiful as far as they are concerned. Huge tower blocks, massive hotels, grandiose tube stations, sixteen-lane city streets.

It was a beautiful sunny day so we decided to walk round. The entrance gateway itself is remarkable, like an Arc de Triomphe, and I recognized the statue on top, the one showing a farm worker and a peasant girl, together lifting up a massive sheaf of corn. You see this image on many Russian cards and posters. It's by a woman sculptress, Vera Mukhina. Moscow intellectuals now consider it a bit naff.

Each of the pavilions is in honour of some activity or product, such as Coal, Agriculture, Science, the Arts, and each building tries to beat the other in the magnificence of its architecture, with classical columns, great pillars, arches and statues. From a distance, I was sure one or two were film sets, grandiose fakes, but they were all real, made of stone and marble from the different Soviet republics.

We went inside a few, but it was too hot and the displays a bit boring and tedious, whereas outside I did at least enjoy the mad designs. I kept on thinking of the Empire Exhibition at Wembley in 1924 – 25, which I never saw, but it's one of my interests and I collect anything to do with it. The Wembley football stadium is about the last remnant, but at one time the site was enormous, with about thirty pavilions from every part of the Empire.

Millions went round it, full of awe, just as they do in Moscow today.

We sat by a large fountain, keeping cool, beside sixteen massive golden statues of women, each representing a different Republic of the Soviet Union. At the far end of the park I could see a collection of aeroplanes, real ones, and a rocket on which I could read the letters BOCTOK, or Vostok as we call it. Wembley was a Wonder, but our Empire never did get into space.

We let Flora off the afternoon's activities, knowing they would not be suitable for her, and half worried that they would not be suitable for us either. Marina and Flora went off in the taxi to find an ice-cream parlour, lucky beggars, while we were dropped off at the offices of a publication called *Soviet Literature*. Svetlana had arranged it, whatever it was she had arranged.

We were shown into a little room, rather bare, a sort of ante-room to a larger office, with a round table in the middle, a big samovar and a plate of Co-op biscuits. I thought at first the samovar might contain some exotic Russian liqueur, even champagne, or a fruit cocktail perhaps, till I saw an electric plug leading from it and realised it was for tea.

There were two men and two women round the table. One of the men was young and dreamy like a tragic poet and hardly spoke. The other was older, bored and tired-looking and seemed a management figure. The younger of the two women had a stick, and was obviously in trouble with her hip. She had a nice smile and spoke English with an American accent, having worked at the UN, but she was overshadowed completely, as everyone seemed to be, by the older woman at the end of the table, Valentina Jaques. She was about sixty, very impressive with swept-back hair, fine features, a strong and powerful personality.

'We hope you will help us and tell us what you think of Soviet Literature,' she said, fixing me with an accusing gaze. 'But first I want *you* to tell us about you. And then we will tell you about us . . .'

She paused, waiting for me to begin. I got out half a sentence, starting to tell her what we both wrote. And that was all. She pounced straight in and harangued us non-stop for the next half-hour. It was an incredible performance. Margaret is normally very good with such strong women, giving as good as she gets, but in a foreign country, and we were supposedly guests, it was hard to know how to react.

Firstly, she attacked us for what Beryl Bainbridge had written in her novel *Winter Garden*, how she had insulted something which Russians take very seriously, the Leningrad cemetery. Margaret eventually came to Beryl's defence, saying you had to realise that Beryl writes black comedy, that's her style, surely nobody could take it as a serious indictment of Russia. But Valentina was not listening, having turned to John le Carré; how he got everything wrong. He had been quite a good writer at first, but now he had gone off, so they had stopped publishing him in Russia.

Then she moved on to Fay Weldon, but this time Margaret managed to turn her on to a more general topic, asking if there were *any* feminist writers in Russia. Valentina said no, there was no need for such things. In Russia all women were equal. Margaret said she thought things were worse in Russia, and they had more need of feminist writing. So many women worked, which meant they all had three jobs – their work, being a mother, running the home. By the sound of Russian men, they did no domestic work at all.

The older of the two men stood up and said we were

being unfair to men, and anyway he had to go, he had urgent work to do. Valentina ignored him.

Margaret meanwhile was continuing with her point about the hard life for Russian women. You just had to look at all the queues. 'There's no need to queue,' replied Valentina. 'You can have things sent to your place of work. I only queue when I need to stock up with fresh stuff, such as sour cream. My husband is very fond of sour cream and likes it with his breakfast.'

But we had *seen* all the queues, with our own eyes. Surely people would not queue if they didn't have to?

'Yes, we do have some problems, but we are working on it. You do not understand the devastation in Russia after the war. Every day we improve a little bit . . .'

My head ached with the concentration needed to listen to her diatribe. Russians are so sensitive, though I suppose that's a sweeping generalisation. Marina could take criticism. Oleg made jokes about himself and his country. Valentina just happened to be one of that breed of heavy Russians we'd met at the Round Table in London, determined to lash out and defend, before they have even been attacked.

An elderly lady in an ill-fitting cardigan came into the room and I thought she was a cleaner, or perhaps come to give us more tea, so I pushed my cup towards her. She sat down beside Valentina, smiled, and then listened for about ten minutes and left. She was a Managing Editor.

I eventually got the conversation round to their magazine, *Soviet Literature*, as I wasn't quite sure about it. Valentina said she was the Editor of its English edition, which she helped to begin, forty years ago. I could well understand her pride. It's published monthly in English, German, French and another six languages, and is meant to cover the best of current Russian writing, prose as well as poetry. One of her jobs was to try to make sure the different Soviet republics were represented. In Britain, it has a sale of about 1,000 a month. Judging by its high-quality printing, full-colour plates, far better paper than in any of the magazines we had seen on the Moscow street stalls, it must be heavily subsidised.

She gave us a pile as we left, getting us to promise to read them and send her any criticism. That made us smile. She'd go mad at any criticism, but I promised I would, thinking I might be stuck for reading material on the long journey south to the Black Sea. When I flicked through them, there did seem a lot of stories set in co-operative farms. Let's hope the journey is not that long.

Our next visit, on our mini cultural tour, was to the offices of the magazine *Inostrannaya Literatura*, or *Foreign Literature*, another publication I had never heard of. Again we were sat down at a round table, with about six editors of the magazine, men and women, but this time each of them was utterly charming and relaxed. Their magazine is the opposite of the other one – they print in Russian, for home consumption, covering the best of world literature in prose, fiction, non-fiction and poetry. It has a large sale of 500,000.

They were all so knowledgeable about modern British authors. They hadn't quite got on to younger writers, like Ian McEwan and Martin Amis, though no doubt their time will come, but they'd run work by John Fowles, *The Ebony Tower*, and even by Tom Sharpe. They were about to serialise *A Married Man* by Piers Paul Read and Graham Greene's newly-discovered old novel, *The Tenth Man*. Each week they read the *Listener, Encounter*, the *TLS*, the *London Magazine, Books and Bookmen* and *Films and Filming*, just to keep up with the British scene.

Oleg, the Deputy Editor, had heard I had written a book about a football team. Why had it never been published in Russia? Russians love football, and would read anything well written about it. Oh, that's what I like to hear. I promised to send him a copy.

One of the women editors, Isabella, told Margaret that her book on Thackeray was already out, which was news to us. It had a rave review in the current *Novi Mir*. Now that is a Russian mag I have heard of. After all, it was the first publication to run Solzhenitsyn. And yesterday on Russian TV, so she said, bits from Margaret's book had been read out. It will be the Russian version of Wogan next, I said. This joke took a lot of explaining, but they all smiled dutifully.

Oleg asked me to write an article for him, on the state of British publishing, describing what sort of stuff was selling well in Britain. I promised I would, as soon as I got back.

It had been so strange, sitting in a Moscow office, talking about the latest British novels, the sort only a few thousand people in Britain read anyway, yet they knew so much, appeared so interested, had been so kind and friendly. Yes, one can't generalise.

Marina took us to the last cultural event of the day in her own car, which was a blessed relief from the wild taxi drivers. As we parked, I suddenly noticed that she had no windscreen wipers on her car. Was this a new Russian invention? Did it never rain in Moscow? She smiled and pulled a pair of rather dusty, worn wipers from a shelf. If you leave them on your car in Moscow, they get pinched.

We were going to the circus. Flora was looking forward to it very much, though I was slightly apprehensive. I don't like English circuses, and I feared a Russian one might be very solemn and serious.

It was the Moscow State Circus, performing not in a tent but in a brand-new permanent site, all concrete and glass, but very artistic, shaped like a Big Top. Inside it was like a massive, modern theatre, with all the latest electronic facilities, more like the Barbican than Bertram Mills, though despite the modern architecture there was a definite smell of horses. Even the RSC doesn't manage that.

The place was packed, with large parties all around us, visiting Africans, soldiers and sailors, tourists and children. We sat beside some Pioneers, members of the junior Communist League, very smart in their white shirts, red neckerchiefs and badges. Very like Boy Scouts, but somehow more innocent and vulnerable.

The attendants were all women, the usual bossy Soviet women, the breed who run lavatories, guard entrances to museums, hefty and dour-looking, who never smile, but this time their uniforms at least were bright and jolly. On the lapels of their jackets I could see splodges of glitter, just to prove we were at a circus, about to enjoy ourselves, rather than be interrogated.

The whole theatre went dark, then several searchlights lit the sky, solemn music was played, and a bloke on a far dais started reciting poetry. Oh, my God. I looked at Flora. Poems at the circus. Very serious, uplifting poetry, by our friend Mayakovsky, praising the triumphs of the Revolution.

I looked round the theatre, and everyone was watching and listening very solemnly. Could they really be enjoying this? I didn't expect anyone to boo, the way some football supporters now do at Wembley during the National Anthem, but I expected to see some trace of boredom. But no, they were all totally respectful. However, when the Circus began in earnest, the whole audience did come to real life and they clapped and laughed and obviously enjoyed themselves tremendously.

The jugglers, Cossack horsemen, animal trainers, acrobats and clowns, were all of such high class, as one might expect from a nation which makes circus performers into People's Artists, but it was all done so imaginatively. It was a combination of the Royal Ballet and the National Theatre, not just simple circus.

Popov, the famous Popov, was a bit of a disappointment. He just strolled through, doing very little, but then I suppose he doesn't have to these days. The other clowns worked much harder. There was a sketch which involved a palm tree and a drunk. The drunk, to avoid being caught, empties his bottle of vodka onto the palm tree – and the tree immediately dies. Moral, don't drink, or you will die.

The palm tree was then removed, so one of the clowns explained, to be taken to the 'vitrezvitel', which resulted in roars of laughter from the audience. Marina explained afterwards that this, roughly translated, means the place where drunks used to go to sober up. Naturally, you don't get drunks in Moscow now, tut, tut, not since good Mr Gorbachev cleaned up the place, but in the bad old days, last year in other words, the police would come round the streets and round up the drunks, then dump them in a special place for the night. They would write to your place of work, informing on your behaviour, then you'd pay a fine and be allowed home. This was the rule all over the Soviet Union, except Armenia for some reason. They didn't have such an institution.

I could have done with a drink at half time, and to hell with the consequences, but it was the usual Russian stalls, selling the inevitable juice and macaroon-type cakes.

The second half was even more remarkable than the first, because at half time, while our back was turned, they had completely transformed the Ring. It all ended with an enormous aerial trapeze show, up in the heights of the theatre, with bodies flying amongst the stars.

There was a message here as well, I think, though I didn't quite get it. Another long poem was recited, attacking any nasty people who might want to use the stars for a battlefield, i.e. the rotten Americans. I think most people just sat back and enjoyed the spectacle. I certainly did.

F. • • • OK, so a circus, you think of conceited-looking ringmasters, barebacked glamour girls with glazed smiles straining in tight glittering leotards, but this circus was amazing and spectacular. It would take too much effort to put it on paper. (La dee da, how pretentious.) It ranged from skate boarding acrobatics to bears. At the interval, the simple-looking circus ring changed into a swimming pool, at least 8 feet deep. Then came synchronised swimming and performing seals. For the finale, the circus was pitch black, as if turned into 'outer space', with luminous stars and planets and acrobats suspended on wires from the ceiling, while the ring itself was turned into an enormous coloured fountain. THIS WAS THE BEST EVENT SO FAR • • •

CHAPTER SIX

Outdoor Pursuits

I'd been trying all week to ring the *Guardian* on the hotel phone. Not the *Guardian*, London, but their office in Moscow. I'd sent their correspondent Martin Walker a letter three weeks previously, saying we were coming, but I'd heard nothing. He'd been in London on an 'urgent mission', so his wife Julia said, rather mysteriously, but he agreed we'd all meet for lunch that day. What fun.

I then went for my morning hot water at the Buffet and Mrs Khrushchev smiled at me. Even the harridans on the corridor, sitting at their little desk, seemed friendlier. Was I breaking them down, or were they just getting used to us?

Marina was waiting for us in the main hall, dressed in her blue blazer as usual, bought from West Germany at vast expense, though she wouldn't tell us how much. Flora thought she'd said it had cost £100, but I couldn't believe it. She was married at one time, now divorced, but we never discovered much about her husband. She lives alone with her cat. She still pounced on all the fashion magazines and English books we could give her. Each morning, I tried to find something lying around which I could bring down for her. She loved horoscopes, something which the

Russian media never feature, and can discuss the subject for hours with Flora. She's longing to go to England, but fears there is no chance. Not just because she is Jewish, but because she's not in the Party. She works as a freelance, doing English teaching, translating, or guiding English-speaking parties around. If she had a full time job with the Writers' Union, it would give her more privileges and help her chances of a foreign visit, but she prefers the freedom of being on her own.

The taxi driver was almost civilised this time, driving nicely for once, so when later he suddenly asked me, when I was on my own, if I could get him a bottle of vodka, from our hotel Berzioka, I said yes. He had to go to a wedding the next day, he explained, but was too busy to queue. I said I'd get one for him that evening. Was I being taken in?

We were dropped off at a little pier, not far from our hotel, on the banks of the river, the Moskva, a tributary of the Volga. It's about the size of the Thames, and a similar muddy colour, with a few barges going up and down, and pleasure boats, but it doesn't have the traffic of the Thames. I suppose the lack of private boats keeps it quieter.

We sat on some chairs beside the pier and waited for the first pleasure boat, admiring all the little Russian girls with their parents. They are all so immaculately dressed with enormous bows in their hair, bright red or bright blue, made of nylon, so big and floppy they are almost like hats.

Our boat had two little decks and held about 100 people, very much like the Thames steamers which go up and down to Greenwich. I went to explore below deck and found a little food kiosk, with the inevitable queue. People must have gone straight to it. It looked more individual than most of the street stalls, but sold the same old stuff – juice, Pepsi, Fanta, biscuits, macaroons. Upstairs, people were taking photographs of the various famous views we could see on the horizon, the Kremlin skyline, the Lenin Stadium, the Lenin Hills.

There was a young Russian couple opposite me, in their mid-twenties, dressed in Western casual wear, jeans and smart tops, expensive training shoes, very well turned out, though I could see they were sweating heavily. They were both a bit too plump for their tight-fitting trendy clothing. He had a most expensive camera and I wondered how he'd managed to buy it. Did he have well-off, middle-class parents who had indulged him? Was he on some sort of fiddle? Perhaps he'd got his camera 'Na lyevo', or on the left, as they say in Russia. What unfair thoughts. They would not have entered my head in the West. I'm sure he had a good job, worked hard, saved his money for his hobbies. Just like anyone else, anywhere else.

We got on the boat at the Kiev Station pier, and got off at the Gorky Park pier, which was neat, names which are known to most of us, East and West, if we read the newspapers. I suppose provincial Russians must be as intrigued by the idea of seeing Gorky Park as we were. I remember coming to London from Carlisle for the first time and dying to visit Trafalgar Square and Piccadilly, mythical names I only knew from Monopoly. Do the Russians have Monopoly? Something else to check.

In the film *Gorky Park*, it was all winter, as I remember, and looked fairly empty, a secluded place in which to hide things, or bump people off, without anyone watching. It was now the height of summer and Gorky Park looked as busy and as popular as Hyde Park, even more so, because I could see a fairground and stalls and other attractions. More like Hampstead Heath on a Bank Holiday. Hard to do anything nasty here, without being seen by everyone. They have ruined so much of Moscow, by clearing away

75

the old districts and throwing up armies of high-rise blocks, but they have left most of the parks. It is almost, if not quite, as richly endowed as London.

We entered through some impressive gates, very like those to the Exhibition of Economic Achievement, and Flora gave a little groan, fearing more pavilions, but we quickly came to the boating ponds and the dodgem cars. The actual garden bits were rather different from our manicured Royal parks. There were flower beds and rose gardens, but not as kempt. The Russian style is to let grass and trees grow free, to give a wilder look than we are thought to prefer in our municipal gardens.

I felt very thirsty and looked along a row of metal cubicles, thinking they might have a new sort of drink, but it was the usual Russian juice. You put a few kopeks in and use a communal glass to drink their revolting sweet water. No wonder the Russians have such awful teeth, drinking this muck all the time. They also have poor complexions, the Russians, when you look at them *en masse*, especially the older folks. Children are the spoiled members of society, getting the best treatment and facilities, in their schools and hospitals and in life, but when they start work, that's it, the cosseting over, it's now bread and gruel. The normal adult diet has so few fresh vegetables or fresh fruit.

Another characteristic, which I had observed after just one week of Russian watching, is the Russian trudge. Walking with Marina was agony as she was so slow. We thought it was just her at first, till we realised that all Russians trudge. They must learn it at school. Then perfect it in the queues. By that time they are slowed down for life.

F. • • • Boat trip to Gorky Park. Pretty boring, full of beautiful little Russian girls who all seem to have their

v. long hair up in plaits with enormous coloured bows and ribbons to match their sweet, but really old-fashioned dresses.

Strolled through Gorky Park at Marina's slug-like pace. It seemed very English, like Regent's Park but had fair-like 'amusements', almost like Blackpool • • •

M. • • • Gorky Park v. lively and jolly, lots of cafés and a funfair. There were huge fat ladies in white coats weighing people on old-style scales for 4K, so I got weighed – 63 Kilos, now how much is that? Flora went to the loo – it won the prize so far for the filthiest loo • • •

Martin Walker had told us to meet him at the Aragvi in Gorky Street, because, so he said, it was the best restaurant in Moscow. He should know. These journalists. I'd last met him two years previously in the Lake District, at the Grasmere Sports. How weird to see him again in Moscow. We had first met his wife Julia even more years ago, when she was still a little girl. (Her father, Graham Watson, formerly head of Curtis Brown, used to be Margaret's agent.)

They were already there when we arrived, along with their daughter Kate, aged 4½, who decided at once that Flora was going to be her best friend. Martin was in fantastic form, smirking because of some journalistic coup. We knew nothing about it, not having read the English press for some time. He'd got a huge spread in the *Guardian* that morning, front page and an inside page, based on a document which had been leaked to him by a top Party official. He never told us which one. He's not that daft, but he did tell us how he sneaked it out of Moscow. In London, he showed it to his editor who asked if publication would result in him being chucked out.

Martin thought it was 50-50, but well worth it. The document contained proposals for various radical changes, such as rival candidates at election time. According to Martin, the *New York Times* had already followed it up, and now every paper in the world was on to it.

I suggested the leak had perhaps been deliberate, to stir up trouble, to make things harder for Gorbachev. He thought not. Well then, perhaps it was Gorbachev's own doing, to make himself look more liberal in Western eyes? Martin still thought the Russians would not be pleased. The document should not have come out, and there would be some reaction. He was due to see his Russian Minder at the end of the week, and there might be some official protest.

They've been in Moscow eighteen months so far, and both of them love it, the life, the people, the country. They both said the winter was best of all. Moscow in the snow was really brilliant and we must come back then to see it at its most beautiful.

Martin had brought with him from London some of the things he usually brings for his Russian friends and contacts – male contraceptives. He has various high-ups who would be looking for them next time he meets them. It's one way to make friends and influence people. The abortion rate in Russia is very high because contraception is either very poor or difficult to get. Most women, married and unmarried, reckon to have six to eight abortions in their life, the highest amount of any country in the world. Under Stalin it was illegal. Now it is the commonest form of birth control.

Julia said she was fed up having them in the house. Martin would stick them away in cupboards and drawers and Kate was always pulling them out when she was playing. She didn't think it was at all amusing.

One of Martin's best contacts is a gynaecologist at one

of the big Moscow hospitals. During the first weeks after Chernobyl, he tried to change the usual Russian exhortations to women, which tells them to drink lots of milk. He wanted them to drink no fresh milk, as it would be dangerous. The authorities refused. They maintained that to do otherwise would cause panic in Moscow.

The Walkers, like all their British colleagues in the diplomatic and media compounds, were still refusing to eat Russian fruit and vegetables, for the sake of their own children. All of it was being imported at vast expense from London, coming through Europe by train. I said I knew two British girls who were stubbornly eating Russian-grown carrots, every morning in fact, the greedy pigs. Julia said she thought visitors would be OK, if they were just passing through.

Living in their compound was their only real complaint about Moscow. All such Westerners have to reside in special blocks, roped off from the natives, well guarded and very hard to enter. They expect to be watched all the time, followed and probably bugged, an accepted part of the job, but it makes their home life totally unnatural. 'It's just like being back at boarding school,' said Julia. Martin thought it was more like apartheid, this awful division between groups.

We were talking so much that I hadn't realised it was now two o'clock, the witching hour. Precisely on the stroke of two, parties of dark-suited, very hefty Russian businessmen trooped in and immediately ordered large flagons of vodka. Martin and I got going on the vino. Oh, it was so nice to have a civilised meal for a change.

I asked him what his next move might be. It always seems strange to me, these foreign correspondents, building up contacts, acquiring knowledge of a country, learning its language, only to move on somewhere completely different. He gave it three years, working in

79

Moscow, then it would be time for a change. 'You go native after three years.' In what way, Mart? 'Oh, you know. Drinking too much, that sort of thing.'

M. • • • Wonderful restaurant, the Aragvi. Cavern-like rooms with frescoes, big heavy tables, almost dungeon-like. Martin in high spirits because of his leaked Russian document. Marina took it all in, silently. Hunt thrilled 'cos at 2 pm prompt the booze arrived. Food by now distinctly familiar: a big 1st course of toms/cucumber/bean salad/ red caviar/garlic and some great Georgian bread like a large doughy pitta. Main course kebab meat, then ice-cream. Julia sd how much they loved Moscow even tho' they feel they live in a ghetto. Any Muscovite who visits them more than once or twice gets leaned on and drops out so it's risky for them (the Russians) to get friendly. They'd have liked Katie to go to a Russian school but it can't be managed. Martin speaks good Russian but she doesn't. He was v. cocky and full of himself, throwing his wt. around with the waiters who seemed to know him • • •

F. • • • Martin has been living here for 18 months as travel correspondent (or something) for the *Guardian* and writes an article on a different aspect of typical Russian life which is very popular. He speaks quite good Russian (according to himself). His lovely extrovert little girl talked non-stop to me throughout.

Quite pleasant hour but boring as I was stuck at the end of the table.

Marina is obsessed with cosmetics and anything to do with slimming, hair, clothes and jewellery and was fascinated with the idea of my 'SUN-IN' and nail-varnish costing just 25p. We can chat for ages on the subject • • •

What a surprise that evening. We not only had a civilised driver, to take us to our next outing, he arrived in a Chaika. Quick, I said to Flora, get the camera out, I want me standing in front of it, won't the folks back home be amazed. The Chaika, meaning sea gull, is one of the two incredibly exclusive cars which are available to top Party Bosses. The other is a Zil. Not sure what that means. But they're both very distinctive, black and enormous and very sleek, a bit like funeral Daimlers. Some of them are bullet-proof, for the likes of Gorbachev, for when he zooms up the middle of the highways, with everyone scattering for cover. We only once saw this in Moscow. We were at a road junction, in an ordinary beat-up taxi, waiting for the lights to change, when a traffic policeman told our driver to wait. He started abusing the policeman, in typical taxi driver way, putting a finger to his ear, cursing and swearing. Then there was a flash of black as a flight of Chaikas and Zils flew past, heading towards the Kremlin. It didn't upset me particularly, or make me feel I was in a totalitarian state. I've had the same experience in Whitehall, being held up by police, just because the PM's car was approaching.

I never discovered why we'd been given a Chaika. I just jumped in, felt the quality, breathed in the space, lay back in the luxury, though it did seem a bit out of proportion, just to go to a football match. If you went to a match in London, in such a posh car, the hooligans would nick your wheels or leave their initials along the bodywork.

The match was in the Lenin Stadium, a bit like Wembley, and it's where they held the Moscow Olympic Games. You know it's the Lenin Stadium because there's a 100-foot statue of him, dominating the entrance. I noticed that one coach was even nearer the front than we were in our Chaika, cheeky blighters, then I slowly translated the letters down the side of the coach, which is a bit hard as the Russians will write their Rs as Ps. I realised it said Torpedo. It was the team coach. Quick, I said to Flora, another photograph. I want me with the lads getting out. She did, but too slowly, and now I look at the photograph all I've got is me standing like a dum dum beside an empty coach.

I decided I had to have a programme and they all moaned when they saw the queue. It was at least 200 yards long, far longer than any British football programme queue. And there seemed to be only one old bloke selling programmes.

I went to the top of the queue, which is always my rule in life, and it was chaos, with boys pushing and shoving, trying to get in. There was a policeman there as well, telling the boys off, but in a very half-hearted fashion. I never actually saw a frightening-looking policeman in Russia, not the sort you get at English matches these days, dressed for a riot, with dogs and helmet shields, looking for someone to thump.

I tried to ask some of the boys if there was another programme seller, someone I'd missed, but my Russian was not up to it. They were too busy shouting and fighting anyway, but one of them suddenly stopped and motioned me to stand there out of the way, then he went back to the scrum. He eventually emerged from under all the bodies with *three* programmes – and gave me one. I offered him the money, but he wouldn't take it. Wasn't that kind? The international brotherhood of football fans.

The programme was only ten kopeks, which is ten pee, and was very flimsy, just two folded-over sheets of stiff lavatory paper, with no photographs, or adverts of course, just a few paragraphs about the two teams, Moscow Spartak against Moscow Torpedo.

I could make out quite a few words as the Russians have pinched many of our Western words for sports, such as, well, 'sport'. Football is football, and they also say penalty, goal, goalkeeper, match. I never found out what sick as a parrot was in Russian, but it's probably very similar.

We had good seats, the best in the stadium, but they were only £1.50 each, the sort you could pay £15 for at Wembley. It's an all-seater stadium and the less good seats are £1. All public entertainment in Russia is amazingly cheap, from the Bolshoi to the circus, at least a fifth of Britain, but then things like clothes cost a fortune.

I looked around the stadium, trying to work out which were the Torpedo fans and which were the Spartak fans. It was a local derby match, so I expected lots of excitement, but they were all very quiet and calm. Not one person in the whole stadium, as far as I saw, was wearing a scarf, a rosette or any sort of football favour, to indicate his team. Nor was there any chanting or singing from the rival supporters. As we entered, they were all intently watching the two teams, Spartak in white and Torpedo in blue, who were warming up.

Not all British teams warm up on the pitch before a match, though I think it's a good idea. Spurs do. Hoddle lets us see his thighs and we all get excited, then they troop back in again. Each of the Russian teams was playing a very intent game of keep ball, forwards against defenders, doing one-touch passing, trying to keep the ball from the other lot.

The match itself began with a hymn. At least it sounded like a hymn to me. A martial bit of music played over the loudspeaker. Marina said it was the tune which introduced most sporting events in Russia. Better than a poem. It was all a bit eerie, with the crowd being so quiet. It was an evening match, and probably only 20,000 were there, out of a possible 100,000. I could hear the players shouting to each other, making more noise than the spectators at times, though the crowd did clap when Spartak got a goal, and there was loud whistling if they didn't like something, such as a long pass back.

At half time, I woke up Margaret and Flora. They hadn't wanted to come anyway, and had only agreed to indulge me. They then spent the rest of the match discussing what things to buy in Oxford Street, when they got home. Marina remained deep in the latest English fashion magazine Flora had given her. It was her first match, and her last, she hoped.

I went to look for refreshments, something I'd never do at a London match. The food is always repulsive and the queues impossible. The Lenin stadium turned out much the same. There were massive queues for Pepsi and the inevitable Russian juice. No alcohol of course. There was some food – stale-looking biscuits and hunks of dry-looking bread with curled slices of salami on top.

In the second half, Spartak scored again, from a penalty, and for the first time I heard some *definite* cheering. I asked Marina what they were shouting and she listened hard and said they were saying 'Good boys'. Oh come on, Marina, surely it's a bit more colourful than that. You must have heard some *swearing*, the odd profanity, but she said no, no swearing.

There were quite a lot of militiamen around, sitting in the front rows, who stood up and faced the crowd at certain moments, such as a penalty, in case the crowds got over-excited.

Towards the end of the match, when Spartak were two goals up and obviously going to win, I did distinctly hear some unison clapping, the first sounds in the whole match which reminded me of Britain. And the rhythm was straight from our matches, as in 'Two, four, six, eight, who do we appree-ce-ate'. In this case, it was Spartak. Perhaps they'd picked it up from the television.

The end of the match was rather weird. It had all been totally good-humoured, no crowd trouble, but we had to file out in strict order, section by section. While we did so, a cartoon film suddenly appeared on the enormous

84

electronic scoreboard. Those waiting to go out were staring up and smiling at the jokes. Flora came to life for about the first time in the match.

The theory, I suppose, is that it will take the crowd's mind off any uncomradely activities, such as tearing up seats or bashing rival fans. Perhaps we could try it in Britain. But I don't really think it would work. Can you imagine Bugs Bunny quietening the North Bank or Tom and Jerry calming down the Kop?

We were not sure if our invitation to Dimitri's was for supper or not, as it wasn't clear on our itinerary. We had been eating bits and pieces all day, so when evening came we didn't feel all that hungry. We left Flora at the hotel, as a reward for good conduct.

Dimitri Zhukov is a Russian writer, translator and a biographer, of a rather academic sort, currently working on a study of Sir Thomas More, so Svetlana had told us. From the outside, his block looked the usual boring council building, no smarter than the rest, but inside it was terribly tasteful, with valuable-looking antique furniture and ikons. I counted twenty in all, plus paintings, some from the sixteenth century. He said he had inherited many from his family and had bought others while they were cheap. Now of course the trade in ikons is prohibited, as the authorities are trying to keep hold of their treasures.

He was tall and handsome, with a military bearing. He had been in the army, until he turned to writing. He and his wife have only one child at home, plus two now grown up. His older daughter was married to a doctor, who he said was probably a genius. 'As a personality,' he said, 'he is as dry as bread.' It was a good turn of phrase. Dimitri's English was not as colloquial as Oleg's, or as easy as Marina's, being much more literary and staid, and it took him time to warm up and get used to speaking English again. He could read it easily, but his talking was rusty.

His wife Irina spoke no English. She was blonde and Slavonic-looking. They made a handsome couple. John Wayne and his leading lady, fresh from Sweden.

He got out the drinks the moment we arrived, wines from Georgia and brandy from Armenia, the sort Churchill used to drink, so he said. I admired all his ikons and told him about the packed churches we had seen at Zagorsk. Presumably he had the ikons for artistic reasons, not religious? 'I am taking no chances.' He was not in the Communist Party, which surprised me, as he had been on various trips to the West which I'd presumed meant you had to be in the Party. He had just had his fourteen-year-old baptised. 'Why not? The Russian Orthodox Church is part of our tradition.'

His wife had made pizza, a Western dish in our honour, which Flora would have liked. We had Russian smoked salmon to start, and delicious apple cake and ice-cream to finish.

The evening was a bit confusing. I couldn't get Dimitri straight. All his affluence and possessions, yet he was simply an academic writer. Not a Communist, yet he'd been in the army as an officer. He travelled freely abroad, yet he was only a writer. A perfect middle-class English meal, in lovely surroundings, beautifully served, first-class wines and brandies, yet we ended with instant coffee and tinned condensed milk, the sort I haven't seen for decades, and hoped I'd never see again. Yes, how can one ever generalise?

F. • • • I got out of going to dinner with another writer, so me and Marina came back to the hotel. She had her feet up and a fag and magazine, while I lay on the sofa with my Walkman • • •

CHAPTER SEVEN

Indoor Pleasures

I've been in quite a few publishing offices in my time, in London and New York, but I've never seen a publisher anywhere with such facilities as Vladimir Kravchenko, Director of Kniga, the firm which that week produced Margaret's Thackeray biography.

She was invited officially to their offices, at 50 Gorky Street, and have her six free copies ceremonially handed over by her publisher in the traditional way. I came along as her friend, in the Denis Thatcher role. Poor Flora had to come because the great Vladimir did not speak any English, so Marina had to be with Margaret to translate. Otherwise, Flora could have sloped off with Marina, eaten ice-creams and discussed horoscopes.

I spotted my first Sloane, sitting in Vladimir's outer office. She was in a two-piece, well-cut summer suit, of a floral design, and looked not unlike a Russian version of Lady Di. We had seen well-turned-out girls before, on the Metro, in the better shops, in our hotel, mostly dressed in casual, sporty clothes, but in all the offices we'd visited so far they seemed to specialise in shapeless cardigans or old-fashioned frocks, belted very tightly round the middle.

She was of course Vladimir's personal private secretary. After a lot of phone-shifting and button-pressing, tossing back her hair, she ushered us into his office.

The room was vast. The walls appeared to be made of black marble with pillars at the end, framing the massive desk where the Big Boss sat, under a portrait of Lenin. I counted five phones – three yellow, two red, plus an intercom machine. As we walked hesitatingly across the length of the room to meet him, he got out his comb, made neat what was left of his hair, then rose to meet us, giving Margaret a great kiss.

Close up, he wasn't all that impressive, in his physique or his clothes. He had on a boring old-fashioned blue two-piece suit and a tie which hung loosely, not quite fitting his neck. He looked rather seedy – but his personality and dynamism shone out. It was obvious, even before Marina started translating, that he was determined to impress us, rolling off facts and figures about his publishing company, gesturing with his hands round his empire.

We went firstly on a guided tour of his own quarters. He had his own dining room and a plush bathroom which he opened and beckoned us inside to inspect, to see the fitted carpet and the gleaming plumbing. Another room was a museum which housed, amongst other things, 2,700 miniature books, from almost every country, he said, one of the biggest, if not the biggest in the world. There was a display area filled with memorabilia, such as Goethe's visiting card, and a sitting room with deep sofas and the latest stereo equipment, all for his own private use. I couldn't quite see why a publisher needed such a luxurious lounge, and suggested quietly to Margaret that it was probably his casting couch, where he interviewed sensitive young lady novelists. Marina did not translate that.

One whole room was devoted entirely to awards – prizes which he had won on behalf of his company, all displayed round the walls. It was a *Citizen Kane* setting, the Hollywood mogul gone mad, though he was more like a little boy, showing off his new toys. It had taken him four years to get his office the way he wanted it. Now, he said, it was just right. His pride was rather touching.

We returned to his main office and he sat with us at a large black leather conference table, big enough to hold splendid twenty-a-side dinner parties. He rang for the editor who had done the work on Margaret's book, a demure lady in large spectacles with very refined English, who came in and lined up with Vladimir, ready to present Margaret with her copies. I felt something special was called for from me, instead of just hanging about being a consort. Flora was being no help, and looked as if she might vomit at any minute. Marina was very harassed, trying hard to keep up with Vlad's endless flow of boasts. I got out my Olympus Trip and made them re-do the hand-over. I never expected any of the shots to come out, as I'd forgotten to bring a flash. (But they did and look rather artistic, don't you think, with that black marble panelling behind.)

Vladimir said he had printed 100,000 copies of *Thackeray*, and we were both suitably astounded. Oh, that was quite normal for him, for a first print. He could have published 500,000, and it would still not have been enough. His firm publishes 1,500 new titles a year and sells 4m copies. It's the third publishing company he has worked in, building it up, and it's now making a profit of 5m roubles a year. That's why we can build such premises, he said, gesturing once again at all his executive toys.

Coffee was produced, and ice-cream which we ate out of special dishes, each of which had the Kniga coat of arms, as did the napkins and other ornaments. He presented me, in my role as m'lady's assistant, with a large package of publicity material which was beautifully printed and lavishly illustrated. He gave Flora a very posh pen, again inscribed with the Kniga logo. I don't think even a top London publisher, such as Hamish Hamilton, has their company trademark on their pens or their dining plates, and they are known in Britain as being very lavish spenders.

Even Vladimir's visiting card was large and ornate, English one side, Russian the other, in very heavy letters, printed like a four-page book. On it, I noticed he was 'A Candidate of Philology and an Honoured Worker of Culture'. There are three grades of Workers and Artists in Russia – Artist, Honoured Artist and People's Artist. You can get these awards whether you are a footballer, circus clown, pop singer, as well as writer, artist or publisher. It gives you great privileges and status.

But, even so, how on earth had he managed all this in a so-called Communist country? There was nothing in socialism, he said, which meant a person could not earn as much as he did. Being cheeky, I asked his salary, and he replied 600 roubles a month. That even made Marina pause. Quite a lot, when the normal professional, salaried person gets 200 to 250 a month. He also has his own car and chauffeur, earns prizes which often come in the form of money, writes articles about publishing which make him extra kopeks, and he was now getting bonuses related to the firm's productivity and profit, which was how it should be. He had a big dacha in the country, which he owned, though in Moscow he lived in the usual high-rise type of accommodation, according to his family size and needs, in his case four rooms, for which he paid thirty roubles a month, all in, including gas and electricity. I suggested he must be saving quite a bit, as his salary obviously exceeded his basic living expenses. 'I like to buy nice dresses for my wife and daughter, that's about all. I do have a big salary, but I would like a bigger one. There are great changes going on in our country now and we will soon be able to expand our firm and do even more things, perhaps one day open our own shops.'

One of his private phones gave a quick buzz and he
stood up to welcome a close-cropped, grey-haired
gentleman who ambled in and was immediately given a
bear hug. Marina knew him at once, a very famous Russian
poet, she murmured, Razul Gamzatov, holder of the Lenin
Award. When Vlad introduced us, he insisted on listing *all*
the poet's prizes, which the poet took in good humour. 'I
collect so many prizes these days that I don't have time to
write any more poetry.'

He looked very interesting, with amused eyes and a
lined rather peasant face, a large nose and heavy lips. He's
from Dagestan in the Caucasus and is also a politician, a
member of the Supreme Soviet, not an unusual thing in
Russia for top poets, who all have great status and
influence.

Vlad himself comes from a peasant family, so he told
us, then he'd gone on to Moscow University. 'Anyone can
do well in Russia,' he said, gripping our hands as we left.
'It just depends on your personality.'

M. • • • Vladimir, the chief director, was so overpowering.
Mighty Mouse himself. Flash office, all stylishly done out,
subtle lighting, frilled muslin curtains, polished floor.
Marina had to translate all his boasts. 'Best publisher in
Russia and everyone knows it.' Hunter tried to interest
him in publishing his biography of Wordsworth, but
without success. We had complicated discussions through
Marina on how a good Commie justifies such lavish
premises and life style.

Svetlana arrived to extract us, hurrah. Flora was by now
reduced to a wreck, near to tears at the thought of yet
another load of Russians yattering over her head, so
Marina offered to take her back to the hotel. Obviously
wanting to go herself and collapse.

Hunt and I then went on our own to Moscow Radio.

Interesting drive thro' a Paris sort of area – yellow painted houses, lots of trees, little park-like areas, the odd church – seemed a long way from the tower blocks. We thought we were just having a tour but it was an interview with a young man called Nikolai – thin, thick black hair, a little beard, quite attractive but v. solemn. He broadcasts from Moscow on a wavelength received in the West. Started off on the London Round Table and what it had been like, then we were on to our impressions of Moscow and then what state England is in today and its literature . . . we sounded real Commies. If anyone who really knows was listening our naivety will drive them mad • • •

We all met up again for lunch at a huge modern complex which we had passed several times and was referred to by Marina as the International Trade Centre, known in Russian as the Mezhdunarodnaya. It was very American, built in 1980, with a glass lift and an enormous entrance hall complete with elaborate fountain. Passes had to be shown to get in, proof of being a Westerner, or that you had permission to work in the Centre. The Russians must find it incredible, at least the handful who ever manage to get inside.

Our hosts were Graham Coe, cultural attaché at the British Embassy in Moscow, and his wife Joan. He presumably felt it part of his duty to lunch visiting English writers. He was small, neat, fussy and wore a bow tie and was very self-assured. Joan was more nervous and scatty, very eager to please.

His Russian was excellent, so Marina told us afterwards, though I could sense it from the way he was instructing the waiters. He spoke standard BBC Russian, whereas Martin Walker spoke it on the run, getting things wrong, and in an obvious English accent, but perhaps in a way conveying more flavour of himself.

92

Graham seemed rather fed up with Moscow, running things down, which didn't seem very diplomatic, then it came out that he had been forced to return to Russia, against his better wishes. I suppose all diplomats, and foreign correspondents as Martin had indicated, grow into a life pattern whereby every three years they expect to be on the move. So to return, for whatever reason, is a bit like treading water, a back projection of what they have already experienced, even in some senses a failure. He'd been in Moscow in the 1970s, as deputy cultural attaché, and then moved on. Six months ago he had been suddenly called back to Moscow, as cultural attaché, which on paper was promotion, but it was due to a sequence of events outside his control. Thirty diplomats had been expelled from the British Embassy, in some tedious tit for tat exchange, and it so happened he was considered the only reasonable Russian-speaking person available who could fill the post.

He seemed a type of Foreign Office person I had met before, who on the surface appears regimented and terribly English, but underneath is seething with resentment and dislikes, if you can ever get them going. He did tell one joke which I wrote down, there and then. Otherwise, I always forget them.

Chernenko, the former Russian leader, had a secretary who was a nymphomaniac. When the very elderly Chernenko died, she was very pleased that the much younger, more virile Gorbachev had taken over. She goes to him one day and moans about her former boss, how useless he was, and asks Gorbachev if he would help her, at once if possible, in the office. Gorbachev hesitates for a long time and then finally agrees. 'OK,' he says. 'But leave the door open. Otherwise they'll think we're drinking . . .'

His wife told a story, a true story, about stopping in a traffic jam in Leningrad where a taxi had broken down.

The taxi driver was a lady and there she was, changing a flat tyre, all on her own, while her four passengers sat inside, three of them men.

Graham ordered special Moldavian wine, hoping I would like it. I said I was longing for any wine, regardless of where it came from. As I leaned forward to examine the label, I noticed a bulge in his inside jacket pocket. A gun? A microphone, recording my inane chat? It was his windscreen wipers. Like Marina, he didn't dare leave them on his car. Marina puts up with it as a boring fact of life, as we in the urban West lock our doors at night, but Graham saw it as an example of Russia's uselessness, its inability to cope with ordinary business life. To get spares for his Russian car, he telexes to Stockman, the Harrods of Helsinki, who send them by train within about ten days. In Russia, you simply can't get anything, he said, not even Russian things.

Neither of them likes the Moscow winters, which the Walkers had raved about. They dislike having to live with the windows closed, to keep in the heat, which means that it's unhealthy, and if visitors arrive who smoke, then it's really awful. They personally could not see all these great 'improvements', the new liberalisation of Russia, which Martin Walker and other Western journalists are now writing about. As far as they could see, life was much the same as it was in the 1970s. 'There are more cars,' he said. 'That's about all.' 'And the people are better dressed,' said his wife.

He admitted, though, there was perhaps slightly more freedom for Western diplomats than before. If they asked permission first, they could usually go to places like Kiev, Leningrad, Minsk, though Siberia was still closed, and any area with heavy industrial or military installations.

In Moscow itself, he didn't feel they were followed as before. 'There are too many of us for them to bother. And they are so obvious when they do. We make a point of deliberately bumping into them, asking the time.' In Lithuania recently, on a trip to a university, they had been followed all the time by a team of large blokes in blue anoraks, easily identified miles away.

I quite enjoyed the lunch, though I could sense that Margaret and Flora were pretty bored, and that Marina did not exactly care for this species of Englishman. He was a knowledgeable, experienced, intelligent chap, yet his opinions on Russia were totally different from the Walkers'. They were of course different personalities, and at different stages in life, but even so, they had such opposite views on the same topic. It's like experts anywhere. You pick your expert, depending on what you want to hear.

And so to the shops, for our last fling in Moscow, hoping we might at least have something to amuse Flora. It won't quite be the same as Oxford Street, I said, or even Camden Lock, but I'm sure there must be some fun places to go where we can buy presents for the folks back home.

First stop was Gum, another of Moscow's landmarks which the rest of the world knows, the State Universal Department Store, situated alongside Red Square. Marina was not keen, saying she preferred local shops, rather than fighting her way through Gum, but I insisted. When in Moscow, do as the Romans.

It was like a series of Burlington Arcades, inside a large two-storey Victorian building, very ornate and splendid, with glass roofs and balconies and little fountains. I liked looking at the people, all looking at each other, but I have to agree the actual stuff on sale was awful. Some attempt had been made at window displays in some of the stalls and shops, at least by Russian standards, which is saying very little, but mostly it was the usual anonymous tins of anonymous fish, piled up in any old order. There were one or two specialist shops selling ties, stockings, jewellery, and Flora queued for a few, just to see what everyone was queuing for, but thought the styles rotten and the prices ridiculous. Most people seemed to be staring, not buying.

Marina said we would do better in Arbat Street, Moscow's smartest shopping street, now a pedestrian freeway, which made it sound like Mayfair or perhaps Covent Garden. It was most attractive, with cobbles and old lamps, bell-shaped umbrellas and flower urns, Georgian-style houses and shops, and little pavement cafés and stalls. As long as you did not look too high up, and see the modern blocks towering in the background, it did look suitably quaint. Even the window displays looked better than the rest of Moscow, but on close inspection the goods were much the same.

In all the guide books, they tell you the good things to buy in Moscow are ceramics, linen, balalaikas, lacquered boxes, fur hats. It wasn't the season for fur hats; as for the other souvenirs, they were all expensive and utterly boring. I had already decided that the only things worth buying as presents from Moscow are the Russian wooden dolls, however corny, and the political propaganda posters. I queued up with a Russian colonel, in full uniform, who was buying enormous posters showing the full Soviet Politburo, all the Members in identical white shirts and suits, well-oiled grey hair and polished complexions. Either the same photographer does them all, or the same touch-up artist. I also bought some more anti-alcohol posters, some anti-religious cartoons, lots of which were pro-peace and pro-Communism, but I could see no anti-Capitalism posters. That sort of crude propaganda seems to have finished.

Flora grew bored rather quickly, with me looking in poster shops and bookshops, as she'd quickly sussed out the clothes situation as being rubbish. I was looking for a café selling coffee when I came across a place which

looked like a German bar, with gothic lettering, selling
something called Kvas. Marina said it was very good, and
I would like it. It was like a real bar inside, with a barmaid
and counter and big pint glasses, but it was the usual
sickly drink. A bit stronger than stuff I'd had before,
thicker and more yeasty, but fit only for sweet-toothed
cattle to drink.

I wanted to queue at Pushkin's house, a nice stucco
building, painted green, rather dwarfed by the skyscrapers
behind, but the queue was too long and the gels very
impatient.

F. • • • Shittiest day so far. Afternoon spent trailing in and
out 2nd hand bookshops and poster shops, led mainly by
daddypoo.

Went to Kniga publishers in the morning who are doing
M's book on Thackeray. Sat in plush board room with
another pain who blew his own trumpet for over 90 mins,
slobbered over mum, which made me feel sick. I sat
bored, tired, and feeling sick while being forced to eat ice-
cream (which could have been nice if I hadn't eaten) . . .
oh, how I love self-pity.

Lunch was in a dreary, formal, stiff, dark restaurant
where we arranged to meet a diplomat and his wife. You
had to feel sorry for the sweet wife who tried so hard to be
interested in us • • •

I had high hopes of dinner. For Flora's sake, not just for
our amusement.

We'd been invited to the home of a very well-known
translator, Tatyana Kudryavtseva, famous in Russia for
her translation of *Gone with the Wind*. Her daughter
Nina, a former member of the Bolshoi Ballet was going to
be there, so that would be interesting. But, best of all,

Svetlana told us that Nina's fifteen-year-old son would also be present, and, by an amazing coincidence, they were both going to be at the Black Sea, in the same Writers' House as us. So Flora would find herself with a ready-made holiday friend, even before we left Moscow.

In honour of the occasion, I put on my Marks and Spencer lightweight blue suit, circa 1969, the only suit I'd brought with me.

The flat was in the usual boring block, but very elegant, with lots of fine furniture, though perhaps not as valuable as Dimitri's. In the kitchen there appeared to be a skivvy, or some sort of cook helper.

Tanya, as we learned to call our hostess, was very dignified looking, but gentle and kind. Nina, her daughter, had recently retired from dancing in the Bolshoi, but was still working for the Company.

I was waiting for her fifteen-year-old son to appear, so I jumped up when the bell suddenly rang. It was another adult guest, Oleg, whom we had met at the *Foreign Literature* magazine. The famous teenage son never turned up. When finally I asked Nina about him, she said he'd gone out of town that night with his father (Nina and the father being divorced). But he would definitely be going to Pitsunda with her, arriving on Sunday. They were travelling by train, she said. I felt a bit cheated. We had been told trains were impossible.

Tanya has translated thirty-eight books altogether – Dickens, Galsworthy, A. J. Cronin, Iris Murdoch, Theodore Dreiser, Richard Aldington, Joyce Carol Oates, John Updike, John Cheever. She found Joyce Carol Oates amongst the hardest to translate. 'She keeps jumping from speaker to speaker, tense to tense, from speech to what the person is thinking, which makes it very difficult.' In Russia at present, she thought the most popular British writers were J. B. Priestley, Graham Greene and more recently Susan Hill. The foreign author who personally gives her most pleasure is Iris Murdoch.

She's a long-standing member of the Writers' Union, as is Nina, who translates books from the French, so we got on to how the Union works. You need to have published two original books to qualify for membership – more if you are a translator. There are 10,000 members, spread across the USSR, with 2,000 in Moscow. It offers four main advantages. You get a very reasonable loan to buy your flat, which you pay back over fifteen years. You get health care. You get sick pay if you are ill, or even if you have a writer's block, which is worked out on your last year's income. Fourthly, you can take advantage of the Union's Rest Homes, such as the one we were going to at Pitsunda.

We then got on to authors' royalties which were a bit complicated. There are no literary agents, as such, so you deal directly with a publisher. They all pay the same sort of rates, so it doesn't really matter financially which publisher you have. The rate is worked out on the number of pages – so many roubles for every twenty-four pages. A normal full-length novel of around 240 pages might give you 3,000 roubles – which can be about the same in England, for a literary novel.

A successful author in Russia, producing a book a year, which sells well, and with a backlog of books still selling, can do very nicely. By my calculations, the top Russian authors must be making £20,000 or more a year, which is very good, when you consider their low accommodation expenses, cheap holidays and other perks, and the fact they only pay thirteen per cent tax if they are on the maximum rate.

I looked round Tanya's flat, thinking of her half-million sales of *Gone with the Wind*, and thought, hmm, not bad, but no doubt at Pitsunda, meeting Russian writers en masse, I might hear rather different stories.

Tanya has travelled quite a bit in the West, and so has

99

Nina, as a ballet dancer, as I quickly realised when I went
to the bathroom. The door was covered with hotel stickers
from almost every Western capital city. It made a rather
pretty wallpaper, just as Oleg, our Professor friend, had a
wall covered in American cigarette packs. If you have
access to the West, it is nice to show it, discreetly of
course.

I'd brought various dopey little presents, but they
seemed a bit pathetic, when they were such sophisticated,
well-travelled people. I had of course expected the fifteen-
year-old son to be there, who might have been more
excited by the cheap biros, postcards of the Queen and
the Beatles. Margaret had brought a bottle of high-class
hand cream. So that was something.

M. • • • Svet picked us up – car had broken down so we
had to get a taxi. Bad-tempered taxi driver who went like
a bat outa hell. Asked him to go slower and he said he had
a living to make.

Same area as last time but a nicer flat – slightly more
spacious tho' v. cluttered. Large table properly set with
china/crystal, etc. Usual 1st course, lumps of meat 2nd
but with delish. mushrooms and fried pots. Tanya a brisk,
quick, thickset lady but witty, not overpowering. Nina
smiling and quiet, thickly made up, ballet dancer figure
and long dark hair tied back. She waited on us, endlessly
directed by her mother. She asked Flora to help at 1 pt
and I wished F had automatically done so – tho' in her
defence it wasn't obvious when to. But once asked she did
well and did it later without prompting. (Tanya leaned
over to say Flora was *beautiful*.) Oleg V arrived after we'd
started – smart in a button-down shirt and a M&S
lightweight suit like Hunt's – who was wearing his so it
looked funny, Tweedledum and Dee, or as F sd. Little and
Large. Good conversation all round – H took down in

minute detail what being a member of the Writer's Union means – and it means a lot, financially and status-wise.

Left at 10.30. Svet cross 'cos Tanya hadn't got a taxi as ordered, saying we'd pick one up easily. We didn't. Oleg V was supposed to get one at a flick of his urbane wrist but failed. Svet had wanted one to take her home direct not just us. So we went on the Metro, F moaning she was tired and hadn't walking shoes on. Svet did at least bring herself to let us walk from the Metro at Kiev station to our hotel alone.

Back at 11.30 exhausted, far too many faces/voices in my head. I think we have done enough in Moscow for one visit. Roll on Pitsunda – except Svet muttered something about our Cultural Tours there. Oh my gawd, all we want is sand and sea and some company for Flora • • •

CHAPTER EIGHT

Black Sea Blues

We were awakened by Marina ringing us at 4.30, then by the hotel switchboard at 4.35, and then by Dima at 4.45, saying he was downstairs, waiting for us in the lobby. The whole world was obviously determined to get us out of Moscow in time and send us on our way to the Black Sea. Marina was not going with us, which was sad. Instead a young man called Dimitri, Dima for short, was going to escort us on the plane and take us to the Writers' Holiday Home.

I had a quick shave, feeling awful at being awake so early, my face not ready for an assault at that time of the morning. I don't think I've been up as early in the last thirty years, not since I had a paper round as a school boy. Flora looked bandbox-fresh, but then she always does, her hair immaculately combed and clipped in place. Margaret had packed our bags the night before, but at the last moment I decided I would take some left-over milk in my hand baggage. I'd at last found a local shop which sold milk in cartons and I'd been keeping it in the fridge all week, for my early morning tea. I also had one bottle of whisky, and two bottles of wine from the Beriozka to take with me, as I feared Pitsunda would have the same ridiculous drinking rules.

Don't be so utterly stupid, she said. You are not taking that milk with you. I've never heard anything so silly.

But there might not be any at Pitsunda. Our hotel could be miles from civilisation. What will I do then?

Do without, she said. Just close that fridge door and hurry up. Dima is waiting for us.

And so, arguing away, we bade farewell to that grand suite in the Ukraine Hotel, our home for the last eight days. I could hear the waterworks beginning to play up as we closed the door. Our Lady of the Corridor was sitting at her desk, her little light on, but dozing, so I walked quietly past, deciding not to hand in my card, but to keep it, as a memento of happy times. Happy? Yes, I'd enjoyed Moscow very much. Most interesting. Some fascinating people. But I now agreed with M and F that we had perhaps done too much, in too short a time, become a bit culture-shocked and exhausted. We needed time to recuperate on a nice beach. If there was a nice beach.

We still had no clear idea what we were going to. Would it be a large dacha, surrounded by smaller dachas? A Victorian villa? Or a modern complex? And would the Black Sea be like the Mediterranean or Blackpool? We'd picked up such confused images. John Roberts in London had said we would be surprised by the luxury of it all, but Katerina, Svetlana's mother, had made faces and run it down, though she did that with lots of people and places. Marina had been that very year, but had failed to convey any real impression of it. Was she hiding something?

It was eerie driving through the empty streets of Moscow in the early morning mist, speeding along by the river, the first rays of sun catching the Kremlin domes in the distance. Our driver was the usual maniac but, with completely empty roads to amuse himself on, the ride was not too bumpy. As ever, he had no seat belt, and smiled to himself as I put mine on. His front windscreen was broken, shattered in a million pieces, but there was just enough clear space in the middle for him to see out. It added to the eeriness. I wanted to ask about the windscreen, but the driver's head was down, concentrating on belting along. Dima said nothing. We sat motionless. It could have been the KGB, an early morning call, come to take us away for questioning.

We arrived at Vnukovo, Moscow's airport for internal flights, which was as big as Gatwick, and looked as busy, with scores of tourists getting out of coaches, but it seemed less frenetic than Gatwick or Heathrow. As foreigners, we were taken through a special Intourist lounge, the first time we had been part of the Intourist set-up, which is the way most foreign visitors to Russia travel, having their hotels and meals and transport done by Intourist guides, although we were still a private party of three, with our own Writers' Union guide, as we'd been all week.

We sat having coffee and cakes in a large, modern lounge. Around us were other Intourist travellers, from places like Poland and Hungary. I could hear no English voices. Dima relaxed a bit more, now that he'd got us safely to the airport. He said he had read my Beatles book five years ago, an underground copy. His dearest wish was to have his own copy. It was a rather heavy hint. I'd only brought two with me from London. One I'd given to Marina, as a farewell present, and the other I was keeping to give to a Moscow publisher at Pitsunda. However, I still had ten *Beatles Monthlies* left, so I gave Dima one. How kind of me.

Our plane was an Ilushin 86, so I read on the side, flight 1015 to Sochi. It was like a Jumbo jet, typical package holiday plane, loaded with tourists, all in their best going-on-holidays casual clothes. They could have been summer-time passengers anywhere in the West.

The plane itself had more room than the British versions and was better upholstered, but the same bland sort of muzak was being played as we took off. There were no demonstrations of the safety belts or oxygen masks. The Russians, despite their image as regimented figures, appear not to bother much with safety regulations. In Moscow, people just cross main-line railway tracks, and ignore safety belts.

The air hostesses were smart and efficient in their blue uniforms, getting everyone organised and settled, but alas there were no refreshments. On such a short internal flight, just two hours or so, all you get is the usual horrible sweet juice, but to my surprise a huge 'Duty Free' trolley appeared, and I got myself ready, thinking I'd be able to stock up on drinks. The trolley was piled high – but with souvenirs, dolls, shampoo, toothbrushes, soap. Everybody seemed to buy something. A young man next to me, aged about thirty, bought a massive soft toy for his little boy who was sleeping on the seat beside him. He unfurled a wad of roubles to pay for it. I suppose the attraction for Russians is that for once goods actually *come* to you. There is no need to go and queue.

There was a blast of warm, Mediterranean air when we landed and I could distinctly see some palm trees in the distance. Sochi is the main airport for the Black Sea resorts, the number one holiday destination for Russians, specially from the northern republics. Almost all of them would be going to official holiday homes, run by their unions. There has been a black market trade for several years in unofficial guest houses, locals letting out rooms at exorbitant rates, to those who had booked too late, or didn't fancy the official union places. Touts would gather at railway stations and the airport, waiting for new arrivals, and say psst, want a private room? This scandal, revealed in the Soviet press, has now been cleaned up, at least made legal. Private guest houses have to register. All part of the new policy to allow some modest private enterprise.

The airport clock showed Moscow time, which airports throughout the Soviet Union use. It does keep things simple. If you had to fly right across the USSR, a distance of 6,800 miles, it could mean going through eleven different time zones. Outside the airport, Dima said we could now put our watches one hour forward, for Georgian time.

I realised we were as much tourists as the other people who had come off the plane, pink and pale and podgy, clean and neat and vaguely affluent-looking. The locals stood out as being much darker, swarthier, untidier, smellier, smaller, moustachioed. But the biggest difference was in their personality, not just appearance. They seemed so noisy, shouting at each other, gesticulating, arguing, laughing, slapping each other's backs. What a change from Moscow. There they had seemed positively restrained by comparison. English even. This was a different country, with its own language, traditions, history. We had been told several times in Moscow that Georgians are not fans of the Russians. In fact they often hate each other's guts. We were now truly in a foreign land . . .

When Flora said that's it, that building over there, I can just tell, I thought it was her little joke, trying to be clever. We were in a little mini-bus, working our way down the Black Sea coast, through lovely little villages, palm trees and pine woods, ever so pretty, ever so like Greece or perhaps bits of Italy, weren't we ever so clever to be going to such an unusual holiday place.

We passed some very attractive villas in a little town, with vines and flowers, pretty gardens, very Mediterranean, and I was becoming convinced we would be staying in something like that, perhaps having one to ourselves, clustered round a central villa, rather faded and splendid like something from Chekhov, or at least 1890s Torquay.

Flora pointed to this big building on the horizon which I couldn't see without my specs. I laughed as we got nearer. How daft to have built such an ugly modern block, right on the beach, in such nice pine woods. Look, there are even three of them, side by side. Yuck. It reminded me once again of that horrible block Caitlin once lived in at King's Cross, a place no one else would live in. Glad we're not going to be anywhere near there, I said.

You've guessed. The mini-bus drew up at the concrete steps of the first tower block. I looked up, half expecting graffiti, thinking still of King's Cross. Above my head were a mass of Communist slogans, all down the balconies at the end of the block. I recognised one of them, 'Miru Mir' which means Peace to the World. (World and Peace in Russian are the same word. Isn't that handy for slogan writers?) Some were in the local Georgian language, rather Arabic-looking.

The block was fourteen floors high, concrete and glass, and inside it was well cared for, nothing flash or luxurious, more like a third-class Benidorm hotel, but adequate for our needs, as was our suite on the sixth floor. Flora had her own bedroom, hurrah, and we had a balcony, a bathroom and a fridge and heh, even a tele. I wonder what Georgian tele is like.

Not bad, I said looking round, what more do we want, really, all that mahogany in Moscow was a bit unnecessary, and so was that piano. This will do us fine. After all, it's the beach we've come for.

We quickly got changed, ran through some luxuriant gardens, and hit the beach. Oh my Gawd, said Flora. I thought perhaps she might cry. There was no sand, just nasty dark pebbles. There was a concrete sort of pier

thing, Solarium as they call it, for use by the Writers'
Union members. Further along the beach were two other
concrete piers, about half a mile apart, for the occupants
of the other blocks. In the first one were journalists from
Pravda. The second was for members of the Screenwriters'
Union. In constructing these three holiday complexes
they'd managed completely to brutalise what must have
been once an attractive beach.

Let's swim, I said. That's *really* what we've come for.
Just ignore the beach. Perhaps Flora did cry this time.
The water was lukewarm, like someone's bath water. And
full of jelly fish.

We returned to our room in silence, had showers and
went down for lunch in the dining room which was large
and sunny and quite well furnished. There was a slight
smell of stale cabbage as we went in, like school dinners,
but our table was in a far corner, by a window, away from
the kitchens. It could be a lot worse, I said, wondering
what worse might possibly be. It is an institution. You
can't expect the Ritz. Dima had disappeared, perhaps
fallen asleep in his room, after the exertions of getting us
here. There were various lists and menus on the table,
like a hospital, where you presumably had to tick what
you wanted for the days ahead. As we sat waiting, I
poured out what I thought was a jug of wine, dying to
have a go at the local Georgian speciality. It looked so
attractive in its jug. It was the dreaded juice.

A plump waitress in an old-fashioned waitress cap came
round and plonked three plates in front of us. Margaret
and Flora refused to have any, but I managed a few
spoonfuls. All around us, families were eating away,
knocking back glasses of the appalling juice. They seemed
such nice people, well-fed, well-dressed, successful,
middle-class families. How could they put up with it? Or
were we just spoiled, Western, capitalist pigs?

F. • • • I'd been looking forward to the lovely Georgian food. Oh my Gawd. All we had to drink at lunch was warm pomegranate juice. There was a salad bar serving carrots, gherkins, cabbage and bread crusts. The starter was re-fried beans, stuck together with a skin that had formed from lying so long. Need one continue . . . Weather was just OK, but a bit hazy and cloudy • • •

M. • • • To complete the horror, the lunch was appalling – sickeningly so. Huge dining room, perfectly pleasant with plants and nice big comfortable red wooden/straw chairs (tho' dreadful close frowsty smell everywhere) but it's like school dinners. They put the first course out – beans re-fried till they gave up – and then trundle round with a trolley laden with utterly yucky glutinous messes – a sort of congealed porridge with fragments of scrawny boiled chicken. Total despair. Not even any water – have to get it from the bar and it wasn't open . . . Flora v. near to tears • • •

In the afternoon, I had another swim, on my own, and it wasn't quite as bad, then I went to explore, heading first of all for the bar. I'd seen it earlier, at least a door marked Bar, but it was closed till eight o'clock. Bloody hell.

I stood around the main reception area, on the left of the front door, seeing what other people were doing, what services might be on offer. There was one woman behind the reception desk, quietly knitting. I noticed a little post office cubicle, with postcards and stamps, and went over, but it was closed. In a far corner of the entrance hall two small kids were watching a programme on TV.

There were no flunkies or doormen or bossy people telling you what to do, which was a relief, but at the same time it all seemed so dead, almost like a sanatorium. With the help of my dictionary, I translated a few of the notices on the walls. 'Drinking Alcohol in the House of Creation is Prohibited.' Oh, Lor. I didn't think it was that bad.

I wandered round the rest of the ground floor and came across a little gym, a table tennis area, and a surprisingly large and well-equipped cinema. I studied a framed notice, addressed I think to the staff. 'Law of Honour – Workers here make your everyday labour a matter of creativity.'

Along the corridor outside the cinema were portraits of the world's great writers. I stood and counted them. Well, it was obviously going to be a long time before the bar opened. They were mostly Russian writers, of course, and I picked out Gogol, Pushkin and Lermontov. Of the non-Russian writers, Britain was the most represented country with four All Time Greats – Shakespeare, Dickens, Shaw and Byron. Byron was a surprise. Didn't think they would have approved of him. The USA was next with three – Hemingway, Dreiser, Mark Twain. France also had three – Balzac, Jules Verne and Exupéry. There was only one from Germany, Goethe, and one from Spain, Cervantes.

Margaret and Flora refused to go down for dinner. Lunch had been more than enough. They didn't intend to eat any meals in that dining room ever again. I hadn't to worry about them. There were some dry biscuits in the case, and cold water in the tap. Tomorrow, they would try to buy some tomatoes. That would do them.

I had my dinner with Dima who was very upset that M and F were not eating with us, seeing it as a reflection on the Rest House. I said no, no, they're just tired. It's been a long day. It was kidneys, which I hate, and a splodge of rice, totally unappetising. Next came a piece of strange-looking fish, which was all bones, then a piece of sponge cake. I managed to eat some of the dinner, just to keep myself alive, while I discussed politics with Dima.

Russia does genuinely want peace, he said, why should anyone in the West disbelieve it? Why does Reagan want Star Wars? Why do you have such horrible films like *Rambo*, stirring up hatred? And why anyway do Western films always portray Russians as bad people? If a Russian is in a film, he is always a spy. Why so?

I am a bit tired, Dima. Give us a break. But he wasn't haranguing me, not like Valentina Jaques. He was simply puzzled, saddened by how the West looks upon Russia. He wanted to understand, not to criticise or score points.

I said well, every intelligent person in the West thinks *Rambo* is rubbish. It's just a pop film. You shouldn't take it seriously. We allow free artistic expression in the West, so we expect sometimes to have a load of old junk. That's the penalty we pay.

As for the Russians being genuinely concerned about peace, what about Afghanistan, huh? Get out of that, Dima. He did look rather pained. It is regrettable, he said.

After dinner, I went to the bar and found it open. It was rather smart, big sofas, disco-type lights, soft music in the background, but all they served was coffee and juice. I bought a bottle of mineral water and a bar of chocolate to take upstairs for Margaret and Flora. They were sitting on our balcony, watching the sea and setting sun. The mineral water turned out to be the fizzy stuff, which Flora doesn't like, you know that, Hunt, and the chocolate was stale. Another failure.

Before bed, Margaret and I had a walk along the front, going onto the end of the Solarium. It was quite pleasant, looking straight out at the Black Sea, taking care to avoid the concrete blocks and piers and cranes along the shore.

Should we go home? On a British holiday we would definitely have checked out by now. The food would have been enough to make us leave. And the beach was not as we'd imagined it from the, well, I can't say brochures, as there were none. We'd painted our own pictures in our

111

minds, expecting a luxury resort, where the top Russians go to besport themselves.

We couldn't really leave. We were guests. It would cause such offence. Russians are so terribly sensitive. Svetlana and Marina had been so helpful, and we liked them both so much. Heads might even roll. We would give British writers a bad name. So we were caught. But how the hell were we going to stand ten days of this?

'It's Flora I'm really worried about,' said Margaret. 'She is so depressed. We wished this upon ourselves, but we *forced* Flora to come. It's not her fault that she has no friends. What are we going to do to help her?'

We then started arguing. Margaret said she only wanted to share her worries about Flora. She wasn't criticising me, but we ended up not talking to each other, walking back to the hotel on our own. Hey ho. What have we done?

In the night, there was a most frightening storm. In our glass and concrete bedrooms it seemed as though we were outside, right in the middle of it, being battered and pummelled. The thunder and lightning didn't just come in flashes but was a constant attack, for over an hour. We ended up all in the same bed, cowering, wishing we were anywhere in the world, except Pitsunda.

CHAPTER NINE

Discovering Pitsunda

F. • • • The bloody weather is really shitty – windy, wet, and cold – not even Dad could pretend it was 'smashing'. Felt very 'depressed' and sorry for meself as I sat watching the rain in the foyer while everyone buzzed around waiting for the bus which was due to arrive at 10 am. Everybody seemed annoyingly cheerful. (Maybe because half of them were going home, as Sunday is changeover day).

Spoke to George who is a Russian publisher who is going to do Dad's Beatles book. He's big with an enormous paunch, grey hair and thickly rimmed glasses who leaves today with his 2nd wife Tanya who doesn't speak a word of English but tried hard. His posh and really loud voice boomed everywhere and he seemed to be the character of the hotel • • •

Georgi Andjaparidze made himself known to us first thing in the morning. It would have been hard not to notice him. Either speaking Russian or English, he dominated the air space, pulling in people for yards around, hands on their shoulders, entertaining them with his stories. Georgi is the first Russian we've met who is larger than life. Vladimir, Margaret's publisher, was a loud personality, but basically just a salesman, a jumped-up businessman. Georgi is a much richer character, a man of the world, suave and assured, intelligent and cultured.

We sat around for an hour, watching Georgi going from group to group, still waiting for our bus. He wasn't going into Pitsunda, but his wife Tanya was. A taxi arrived, dropping off some people at our hotel, so I said to Margaret, quick, let's get it, I'm not sitting here all day. Russians are used to waiting.

I kept the taxi's door open, and tried to explain what I wanted, but of course the driver was Georgian and didn't understand my pidgin Russian. Luckily Tanya and another lady came forward and all five of us crammed into the beat-up old taxi. As we drove out of the hotel gardens, the hotel mini-bus arrived. What the hell. Spare no expense. We are on holiday.

The driver looked like Stalin's grandad, with a huge droopy moustache. His taxi was a mess, bits hanging off, panels missing, straw and dirt all over the floor, gears that looked as if they would come to pieces, but he was very jolly, laughing away, smelling heavily of local cigarettes and garlic, driving wildly with one hand on the wheel.

We were heading for Pitsunda's open air market, on the outskirts of the town, about four miles away. It was terribly genuine, rough stalls under corrugated iron roofs, old peasant women in black with headscarfs and young Georgian blokes, unshaven and leering. It was a refreshing change to be openly stared at. In Moscow it appeared as if we were being ignored, though if I ever fell behind I could tell that people were in fact looking at M and F. We met other people from our hotel and they rushed to help if they saw us having trouble with the prices, pointing out the best, helping us negotiate. It was rather overwhelming, their desire to be kind.

The prices were still expensive, compared with British markets, but they were half that of Moscow. I saw some nice roses, and thought about a bunch to cheer up the girls, but they were £1 each. Instead I bought a small melon for only £2 and a kilo of plums for £2, plus lots of tomatoes and some cheese. There were several shops round the edge of the market, a little café, and a couple of dress stalls, selling the usual Russian women's wear – street market 1950s style, and all very expensive. A cheap, simple frock, perhaps £7 from a Camden Town street stall, was £70. Tanya, despite her lack of English, pointed out to us some local herbs, done up in little bunches, a parsley type and a sort of mint, so we bought some.

The hotel mini-bus came to pick us all up after an hour. It was obviously a regular run, taking writers from the Rest House to stock up on ancillary supplies, to make the dining room food more palatable. Perhaps things were slightly looking up.

As we got off the mini-bus, one of the ladies from our hotel presented Flora with a large bunch of red roses. I'd never spoken to her before, and she disappeared into the hotel before we could properly thank her.

We tried sitting on the beach itself, on the pebbly bits, but it was hellish uncomfortable. There were little wooden beach rafts, painted green, which were available for lying on, so I carted three of them over for us to use, but they were very hard. So we decided to go on high, to the top deck of the Solarium. It looked ugly from below, but was quite pleasant under the sun awning.

Georgi was already there, surrounded by an admiring gang, listening to his stories. He complimented me on my tan, and I said it was nothing, just my Celtic blood. We had in fact been to exotic places twice quite recently – to Barbados in January, to celebrate my fiftieth birthday,

115

and then to California at Easter to visit Caitlin. I didn't want to admit all that, not to Russians who are not allowed anywhere. Rather flash. In turn I admired Georgi's tan, which was very good.

'Oh, this is my third holiday in the sun this year,' he said. 'At Easter I was in Cuba, and then in May I was in California.'

That put me in my place. He'd been on a conference in California and doing publishing business in Cuba. 'I have three rules as a publisher,' he said. 'One, I publish books by my friends. Two, I publish books by pretty girls. Three, I publish books which mean I have to travel abroad in the sun.' Everyone laughed. I realised then how many people did speak English. Enough at least to understand it, even if they were obviously a bit hesitant about trying it out with their first real live Brit.

Georgi had sunbathed on the Solarium, in the same corner, every day, morning and afternoon, for the last twenty-four days. No, he hadn't been bored. He lived a hectic life, so he needed to relax completely. Perhaps now he was ready for Moscow again.

I asked him as tactfully as possible about the food. We'd just arrived, and I had had only two meals, but were they, eh, all like that? He looked at me carefully. 'What is wrong with the meals? I think they are perfectly adequate. Hearty, I think you English would call them.'

I could sense a bit of steel in Georgi. Behind all that bonhomie and jokiness, he might be another sensitive Russian soul, easily upset by any criticism. In Britain we're so used to running each other down, mocking the country, laughing at all the awful things going wrong, that I always find untarnished patriotism rather a surprise. In America, it was even worse.

But, there again, Georgi was a cosmopolitan, been around the world, eaten in the best places, could he *really* like the awful food? Perhaps we were the hicks, moaning because there was no muesli or fresh grapefruit for breakfast, no percolated coffee or croissant, nor a tossed green salad and a bottle of Soave, or any of the other essentials of our insular, NW5 life.

I invited Georgi and his wife to have a drink with us in our room before he departed. I wanted to give him my Beatles book.

Oh no, what have you done, said Margaret, as I sat down beside her and laid out my towel. We've got nothing to give him. We can't make tea or coffee in our room as there's no kettle. Whisky, I said. Georgi looks the sort of bloke who'll like a glass or two.

I also invited Dima, who was going back to Moscow that day. I asked them all what they wanted, boasting that I did have some real Scotch whisky. Georgi said yes at once. Tanya and Dima said they would prefer tea. I produced our best Waitrose tea bags, and also some Waitrose fresh coffee, but explained I had nothing to make it in.

Georgi said something to Tanya and off she scuttled, returning with an electric lead. On one end was a plug. On the other a bare element. 'Never travel without it,' said Georgi. He got a milk jug from our cupboard, filled it full of water, put the bare element in the water, switched on, and in four minutes it was bubbling merrily away.

We discussed Melvyn Bragg, whom he has published, Iris Murdoch, whom everyone publishes, and also Graham Greene, William Golding and James Aldridge. The Russians do seem very fond of Aldridge, a writer hardly known in Britain. Tanya was rather out of all this, and so was Dima. I watched his face to see what he might think of Georgi. A middle-class Moscow smoothie?

Georgi said he would invite us for dinner at his apartment in Moscow, on our way home, if we had time. I

117

didn't quite know our timetable, but I asked him to ring Marina on his return to Moscow. It would be great to see him again. Especially if he is going to publish *The Beatles*. Oh yes, he said, definitely, just a few things about the money and the contract, but let's not spoil a holiday by talking business.

Later in the afternoon, we went down to the front hall to see them off. It was nice that we had overlapped, but one day was very short, and it was rather sad to see them go. He was so entertaining, with such good English. He knew everybody and knew his way around. The hotel felt a bit empty without him.

Almost as soon as they left, Nina and her son arrived, the one we had failed to meet in Moscow. Nina looked older and far less glamorous than she'd appeared in Moscow at her mother's dinner party, which wasn't surprising. They'd had a hellish two-day train journey from Moscow, unable to sleep, no food, very uncomfortable, and they'd been in a thunderstorm for miles, the one which had terrified us.

There, said Margaret and Flora, thank goodness we didn't come by train. I presume now that the real reason we hadn't been allowed to was not because of any Chernobyl scare, but because nobody from the Writers' Union would agree to accompany us, knowing how lousy a long Russian train journey can be.

I invited them to have coffee with us, once they'd unpacked. It was probably a bit forward, as they were obviously exhausted, but I so wanted Flora to make a young friend. Nina's fifteen-year-old son Lorka, at least that's how it seemed to be pronounced, did look very pleasant. I had feared he might be a little weedy swot, with specs, not that I have anything against weedy swots, or specs, but Flora is tall for her age and it could be embarrassing for a fifteen-year-old boy to look younger

Our Moscow Hotel, the Ukraine: 29 floors, 1500 rooms, very little to drink.

Marina, our guide, Flora and Hunter, at the exciting Exhibition of Economic Achievement.

Flora, Margaret and Marina in Red Square, amidst the admiring girls from Tashkent.

Marina, Flora and Margaret pose for every Russian's favourite snap – outside St Basil's, Red Square.

Les girls again, with more girls behind, statues from the Soviet Republics at the Econ Achievement Exhib.

Zagorsk, the religious capital of Russia: God fights back.

Off in a Chaika to a football match: Mammon moves in.

Margaret and Flora, rather theatrical, in Gorky Park.

Rita Puskin, Beatles fan club secretary.

Margaret with the famous poet,
Gamzatov.

Black Sea at last: note the loyal slogans on the Writers House.

The Writers beach: note the concrete block.

A Black Sea café: notable for the bell shaped umbrellas.

Fellow Writers and
Fishermen, Albert and Hunt:
Spot the shark.

Georgi, the famous publisher, fresh
from Cuba and California.

Flora and her friend Fatsima from
Tashkent.

Two poets: Ataol from Turkey,
Alba from Nicaragua.

The market in Pitsunda: very Georgian.

An octopus shaped bus stop: very strange.

Writers on the Writers beach.

Fyodor, the Boy Wonder and
Beatles brain.

Lorka, our constant friend, in
denim and UK T-shirt.

than she does. He also looked modern, a distinct advantage in Flora's eyes, wearing a denim jacket and an English T-shirt. Would they hit it off?

M. • • • Lorka looks young for Flora but attractive and tall – not sure if he'll be of any use to her tho'. Anyway, Hunt brought them back for coffee – wot a palaver this is 'cos he had to borrow their magic lethal looking gadget to heat water and then he slutters around with the coffee warming cups – people can't really cope with all the hassle all for a miz. cup of coffee. Nina talks French, Lorka attempts Eng. – it's all v. awkward and stilted and tiring and hard to really get anywhere.

F. • • • Lucca or Lorka (I prefer to pronounce it 'Look-ca') is supposed to be my boy/friend for the next 10 days, (so they imagine). I think he is 15, quite tall, brown/blond hair, blue eyes, nice eyebrows, and speaks quite good English in a lovely Russian accent. Spent half an hour while dad faffed around making coffee and silly comments like – 'Lucca likes heavy metal, don't you? Flora, why don't you show him some of your Sade tapes?' (Groan) Nina and dad made stilted conversation while me and Lucca nodded and pretended not to be interested in each other.

Went with him to the packed and hot little cinema in the hotel at 9 pm to watch *Salamanda* which is American but of course was dubbed in Russian. Left after twenty minutes.

Met Alba for the second time, a friend of Georgi's. She's a Nicaraguan poet who speaks Italian, Russian, French and Spanish but no English.

Lovely and cheerful so had a funny conversation with

119

her in mixed languages plus the odd bit of English, then came back for my delicious meal of tomatoes.

Met a guy in the lift who shook my hand and said his name was Alex and he has studied English for 11 years at school and his room number was '220 without one' (in other words 219! ! ! !) • • •

While Flora went off to the pictures with Lorka, to see some American film, I went for a walk into town with Sasha Bransky. He was to be our unofficial minder during our stay in Pitsunda. He works for the Writers' Union in Leningrad and was on holiday with his own family, but at the same time he was supposed to be looking after the handful of foreign guest writers. We were the only Westerners, so he'd told me, but there was the Nicaraguan poetess, Alba, whom Georgi had introduced us to, and some Czechs were rumoured to be on the way.

He was small with a beard and looked very worried and lost, and didn't seem to know his way around any more than we did, though on a beach holiday, as opposed to Moscow, we obviously did not really need anyone. We'd already been told we had complete freedom to go anywhere, do anything we liked, or do nothing at all.

Sasha's wife and son decided to come as well. She was Armenian, dark and quiet and spoke no English. Their six-year-old son Toamy was the one with all the energy and noise. Strange how such a lively little lad had come from two such stolid parents. He ran rings round us the first mile, jumping about, non-stop talking, in Russian and in English. He had a flow of pretend English, just as Flora used to have, plus some real words, grabbing my arm and saying, 'Hello Goodbye How Are You Thank You Very Much,' all said as one sentence. Then he would dash away, thrilled with his own jokes. Sasha gazed at him indulgently. I thought at first it must be their only child, but they have a twenty-three-year-old son at home, recently married, which Sasha wasn't so pleased about, as he and his wife are still students.

About half-way to Pitsunda, Toamy's energy ran out, as was to be expected. We experienced fathers know the signs. Sasha carried him for a bit, then his mother decided to turn back with him, and let us go on alone.

So I got Sasha's life story. Born in Leningrad, father died in the war in the siege of Leningrad. Left school, became a radio operator, then went as a part-time mature student to Leningrad University to study English. Worked for Intourist, then the Writers' Union where he now looks after their foreign section. They have only 400 members in Leningrad, compared with Moscow's 2,000, but it's very active and important. He has translated two books into Russian, one by Agatha Christie, but to become a member of the Union, as a translator, you need five books to your credit. He didn't know whether he would still be able to work for the Writers' Union, if he ever became a Member himself.

'Twenty-five years ago, at the Writers' Union Rest Homes, things were much more regulated. There were group leaders who made you do exercises, turn out for volleyball, attend classes all day long. Now people are left to their own devices.' Sasha rather regretted the changes. He thinks people on holiday do like things organised for them.

In the old days, there was a lot of drinking, especially in people's rooms, but he didn't think that happened now. People obey the new laws. He personally did not drink vodka, but he missed being able to have a bottle of wine a week, or when friends came to his flat for a meal. 'Now I have to queue three hours for this harmless pleasure.'

We passed lots of notices and road signs as we neared Pitsunda. Many were written in three or four languages – Abkhazian, which is the local language, Georgian, the official language of the Republic, and Russian, the official language of the Soviet Union. And in many cases the Russian word, in the Russian alphabet, was followed by the same word, using Latin letters. This is not to help the Western tourists, as there are so few on the Russian Black Sea coast, but to help Communist Block tourists who perhaps are more used to Western lettering.

As we got into the town, we met lots of smartly dressed tourists, from Poland and East Germany, and also the Soviet Republics. As in any holiday town anywhere, the tourists stood out sharply from the locals. I had an ice-cream in the central square, where the buses arrive, and admired an old Russian Orthodox church, now a museum. There were the usual hideous tower blocks around the edges of the town, but the middle was green, with low-level shops and buildings, a few old houses, rather like an American small town.

I noticed a couple of supermarkets still open, so I rushed over, telling Sasha to wait. No wine, no beer, nothing. At the next shop, I sent Sasha, telling him to find out if there was any wine shop in the whole town. Only one, he said. Let's go, I said. It took us ages to find it, right on the other side of the town. It was on the ground floor of a dusty, decaying tower block, surrounded by rubble and junk. Yes, that is the wine shop, a man assured us. I banged at the dirty window. It was closed. It opened only a few hours a day. I memorised the times, determined to crack it, before we left Pitsunda.

Back in the hotel, I decided I'd have a late-night cup of tea, so I went down to the dining room, with my empty tea pot, thinking one of the waitresses might let me have some hot water from one of their massive samovars. I knocked at the glass door, trying to attract the attention of a lady cleaning up, but she ignored me.

As I stood there, a very attractive blonde girl, wearing flimsy silk shorts and an 'I love NY' T-shirt, asked if she could help. I explained my problem and she said she had a plug in her room. Follow me.

I went up in the lift with her. Her English was terrific, with an American accent, though she had never been to America, or England. The accent came from watching American films. I said she looked a bit young to be a member of the Writers' Union, and she smiled and said she was a student. It was her father who was a writer. They came here every year.

We got out at her floor and walked down a long corridor. How kind of her to bother. Or was it a trap? I'd not had suspicious thoughts of KGB men since leaving Moscow. The atmosphere was so relaxed that we might well have been in Spain or Italy.

She got out her key, opened her bedroom door and beckoned me in. There was a scurry inside, and a half-naked middle-aged couple practically jumped in the air, but then so would I, if a strange man had suddenly entered our bedroom. It was a one-bedroom apartment, nowhere near as spacious as ours, and the girl and her parents were obviously sharing it.

The father gave her a mouthful in Russian, and she presumably explained that all she wanted was the plug for this Englishman. He stopped and stared at me, amidst his cases and clothes strewn everywhere. They had just arrived from Moscow, so he said to me in English. Perhaps if I called tomorrow, at a more suitable time, hmm? Then I could borrow their plug. Thank you very much, goodnight . . .

CHAPTER TEN

Routine Activities

It's odd how a holiday routine imposes itself. One minute you are a complete stranger, unable to know what goes on, a gauche little first former to whom everything is strange, and then the next moment you realise this is what we always do, this is where we always sit, at this time every day we have our Hachipuree. In just a few days, you can convince yourself you've been in the sixth form for ever.

After those initial feelings of horror, we became quite fond of the hotel, as we preferred to call it. 'Rest Home' sounded so institutional. Every morning, Margaret and I had a pre-breakfast swim, though Flora rarely did, feeling too tired, so she said, or just being lazy. It was the nicest swim of the day, so refreshing and calm, a slight haze on the water looking across to Turkey. Is it Turkey? Must study the map again. Overweight Russian ladies would waddle down in their brightly-coloured beach robes, unwrap themselves like ships being launched, then float out a few yards, and just lie there. There was one who always wore a large turban on her head, orange and white, and I took this floating object to be a buoy, the first time I saw it, and I said to Margaret, I'll race you, last to touch it is a sissy.

At breakfast time, Margaret and Flora had a piece of bread and cheese in our room, while I went to the dining room. I stuck to bread and tea, plus now and again a boiled egg, though it was always cold by the time it arrived. As Margaret and Flora were determined never to darken the dining room again, Nina and Lorka moved to my table. Nina always brought her own instant coffee, sometimes her own honey, and ate very daintily, but Lorka ate for Russia, polishing off all the horrible dishes provided, drowning them in the special Georgian sauce he'd bought in the market, very popular with all the Russians.

Then we had the morning on the beach. We always sat on the top deck of the Solarium, in the same chairs, in the space vacated by Georgi, but Flora preferred to be down on the beach where there was more action. We were not sure what the action was but, after our worries of that first day, she seemed to be occupied most of the time. Though not with Lorka. He turned out to be my friend. Always available to chat with me, swim with me, and walk into Pitsunda in the evening, if I wanted a companion.

The beach always cleared at lunch time, till about four, but we never left. We at last sussed out the mystery of the little bar beneath the Solarium, and the strange dish we'd seen people eating on the first day, Hachipuree. I never saw it written down, so I'm not sure how it is spelled. It's a local Georgian version of pitta bread, but soft and doughy, filled in the middle with sour cheese, topped with melted butter. They made it on the premises, so the queue was vast when the next load was due out of the oven. Most people ate it for their mid-morning snack, before going off for lunch proper in the dining room. We waited till near one o'clock to have ours, watching the queue below through the bars of my sun chair, timing it so the crowds

125

had gone, which was difficult, as there was no logic to their opening hours, then I'd rush down and buy three Hachipuree and bring them back to the sun deck.

We had them for our lunch, with a little salad, made from our market purchases, and I also had a miniature bottle of wine each day. I'd managed to get two bottles from the Pitsunda wine shop at last, and I'd decanted them into my aeroplane-size wine bottles I'd brought with me. What bliss. I did enjoy those lunches.

Then if I was lucky, and had timed it well, I finished off with a cup of real Turkish coffee. They did this on the premises as well, which makes it sound like a proper café, but it was simply a large concrete room, totally barren, with an oven for the bread and a tray of hot ashes for the coffee. This is the Russian style of coffee-making I'd noticed in Moscow. Hot water and coffee grounds are put in a little long-handled copper jug, enough for one small cup, then it is held out over the hot ashes, moving it around, till it all fuses and makes the thick, smooth Turkish coffee. It's an elaborate process, and only about three cups can be done at a time. I suppose they do something similar in Greek restaurants in London, but I've never been behind the scenes. In Russia they make it on the counter, in front of you. Very visual, almost mesmeric, as they go through the ritual, as if in a trance.

The bar then closed about half past one, and that was it, for the rest of the day, even though their notice-board said it was open till eight in the evening. Yet there was obviously a big demand for their excellent coffee and wonderful Hachipuree. The woman who served, and a man with one eye who was the baker, were both presumably on the staff of the Writers' Hotel. I suppose, like all Russian workers, they were given a target, so much food to shift a day, and that was it. So they closed when they'd done their bit.

There was nothing else on the beach, no kiosks, no

stalls or anyone selling anything, either on our beach or the adjoining two beaches, yet every day there must have been at least one thousand people on our one-mile stretch. I know in the Med. it can get out of hand, with people trying to sell you junk round the clock, but an ice-cream would have been nice. The Russians moaned just as much as we did when the bar suddenly closed, but they all accepted it as a way of life.

I was given the same old story whenever I put this to people, that things *were* getting better all the time, a certain amount of private enterprise and individual initiative was now being allowed, but in our experience service was generally terrible. I'd expected Georgians to flout all the petty Soviet rules, and go their own way, but I didn't see much sign of it. In Pitsunda the shops were as boring and dreary and unattractive as in Moscow.

One theory why the economy generally is in such a bad way, and not just in small-scale things like shops, is because for so long the country's best brains have gone into either science or the army, which has resulted in Russia having the world's biggest army and a lead in space research.

Centralised State control, with endless targets and plans dictated from Moscow, will always make it hard for the consumer business, which is why some sort of controlled capitalism seems to be coming in. Now that they have got their space ships to run on time, perhaps they'll put their great brains to the problem of getting Hachipuree, and other ordinary pleasures of life, to the customers, waiting so patiently in their queues.

We had a meeting one morning with the Director, which seemed to sum up the Russian hierarchical system, everyone scared to take any initiative.

All the foreign guest writers were told to assemble outside his office at ten o'clock. We sat in his corridor, not talking, as if waiting for the headmaster to see us, with Sasha hovering around, looking worried, the head prefect who was responsible for our behaviour, but who himself might be given lines. We were eventually shown into a very large room where the Director sat behind a sequence of pine desks, which could be moved around to make one big desk, for really big meetings, but the way he had it arranged, it looked like a barricade, separating him from the underlings. We were lined up against a wall on hard wooden chairs, eight of us in all – me and Margaret, Alba the Nicaraguan poetess, a poet from Turkey I hadn't seen before, two from Hungary, two from Czechoslovakia.

The Director addressed us in Russian, which everyone else could understand, except me and Margaret, so Sasha leaned forward, in hushed and reverential tones, and whispered the translation, as if it were pearls from the Pope's lips, rather than the history of the Writers' Rest Home. It all began in 1932, when the Union had five rooms in Gagra, the next town down the coast. It grew big enough by 1950 to hold 150 writers. Their present building was begun in 1967 and has been in operation ten years. It accommodates 500 writers and their families. People come for twenty-four days at a time, that being the normal duration of Russian holidays. It also opens in the winter, but they're not as busy. In an average year, there are 5,000 guests, 3,000 being actual writers, the rest families.

A writer pays only 140 roubles for the twenty-four days, his wife or adult members of his family 200 roubles, and his children get half price, any questions. Nobody had any questions. In a corner, throughout the Director's speech, a young man was sitting taking notes. He didn't look like a clerk, as he was wearing a red satin track suit top, very chic. A male secretary? Head of games? A Butlin's Redcoat?

I avoided Margaret's eye, in case we started laughing. All the other guests looked suitably solemn. Only the

Turkish poet, a man of about forty with a large interesting moustache, was making no effort to conceal his boredom. He leaned over to me and said, in a loud whisper, that he was a friend of Adrian Mitchell's.

The Turkish poet later introduced himself properly, Ataol Behramoglu, and he became one of our Solarium friends, chatting on the sun deck each day.

He is based in Paris, having been forced to leave Turkey, after a year in a Turkish prison for political activities against the government, which mainly seemed to consist of joining a peace committee.

I said it must be awful, a year in a Turkish prison, reputedly the worst in Europe, according to the film *Midnight Express*. He said that film gave a false impression of Turkey. There are some bad places, as there are in any country, but he was not ill-treated. 'As a member of the intelligentsia, I had fairly good conditions.' He was allowed out in the end, on condition that he left the country, so he chose Paris, a traditional refuge for émigrés, with a large Turkish community. He manages to live by giving lectures, reading his poems. He'd recently done a lecture tour of Australia.

He and Flora were the only two people on that whole Black Sea beach with Sony Walkmen, much to the envy of all the Russian teenagers. He bought his at London Airport, after giving some poetry readings in London. Which is how he'd come to meet Adrian Mitchell.

His wife and daughter were also with him, but they seemed to stay in their room most of the day. She was blonde, while he was so dark. He said you often got blonde Turks, thanks to the Ottoman Empire. A lot of Slav and Russian blood had got mixed up in Turkey.

Once again, I felt so pathetic, unable to speak to people in their own language. Here we were, sitting in Russia, with a Turkish poet, based in France, who was conversing with us in fluent English. All our intercourse depended on people addressing us in our language. Yet how can you know people when you rely on them to take the lead in a one-sided dialogue? If not, there is nothing. Just a headache, trying to concentrate on sign language or pidgin talk.

F. • • • Two of Lorka's schoolfriends have arrived, very polite and smiley. So I retired to the sea while daddy came down and enjoyed himself talking to them in their very good English. I hardly speak as I can never think of much to say. How pathetic.

Hunt has met a few friends and showed them his copy of *Punch* which they 'surprisingly' loved, to his delight • • •

As I looked down each day from my sun chair on to the beach, usually to see if there was a queue for the bar, it seemed to me that Flora was gradually becoming the centre of an admiring group, with people constantly around her, young and not so young. But she was kind, not wishing the wrinklies to be left out of things, and from time to time people started coming up on top of the Solarium and shyly saying hello. Flora had sent them.

The first person who came and chatted, saying he had met Flora, was a journalist called Vladimir from the *Pravda* building. Although the three blocks were separate, about half a mile apart, and had their own gardens, tennis courts, bars and dining room, there was free access between them, on the beach and through the gardens. He said he wanted to interview me for a magazine, so naturally I agreed.

The magazine was called *Ogonek*, or little flame, a news feature magazine which comes out once a month and sells 1½ million copies. There was colour on the cover, and not much inside, and the paper itself was very flimsy. He brought me the latest edition, with an article by him, an interview with a Spanish guitarist. Flicking through, there seemed to be a lot of photographs of the last war, showing once again the Russian obsession, but he said that was chance, the film of the week happened to be a war film, and the main feature happened to be on Poland. There was a long article on a model town in the Ukraine, where a new experiment in socialist-capitalist economy is under way, with the money from the factory not going straight to the State, in the normal way, but back into the factory, in bonuses and expansion. It hadn't been operating long, so there were no clear results.

Vladimir's wife was with him, a school teacher, earning 250 roubles a month, which was more than he earned. I was surprised. In Britain, I told him, national journalists get at least double what teachers get. He was on only 200 a month, despite having been to an Institute in Moscow and done eight years as a journalist. They've been married five years and have a little boy, Dimitri. They live in a three-room flat which they are buying at a cost of 6,000 roubles. They'd borrowed money from the State Bank. Out of their combined income per month of 450 roubles, about 50 went in tax, 35 to the Bank, 100 on food, 100 on clothes, and he wasn't sure where the rest went, but each month they saved 50 roubles, which went towards their annual holiday.

I was surprised to learn you can 'own' your flat, buying it from the State, though you can't sell it to another person. You can leave it to your child, if that child is still living with you. If the child already has a flat, then two flats cannot be owned, so it has to be sold back to the State. The dacha, or country cottage, system has more flexibility. A family can own one for ever, and you can inherit one, even if you already own a flat in town.

131

I hope I've got that clear. Vladimir's English was not perfect, so I soon had a headache, trying to understand it all, as I'm sure he had. Time for a swim, Vlad. I am on holiday.

M. • • • This evening we walked along the beach with Nina and Lorka and another of Hunt's journalist friends, Dima. On the edge of 'getting heated', so we sensibly stopped. On the way back Dima discussed Afghanistan. Lorka left them and caught us up: he doesn't want to die in Afghanistan for a reason he doesn't know – he didn't like Dima saying Russia was *right* to be there ('Dima is too old to serve himself and he's only got a daughter').

Poor Lorka. Nina says he's jealous of Flora's new friends – he also apparently says Flora doesn't know how to relate to him 'cos she goes to an all-girls school.

Then Nina invited us to her and Lorka's room 'for 9 o'clock' – had to say yes. Flora was out, so we went alone. So sweet – little table from the balcony set with plates of sliced tomato/cucumber/rolls – even tho' it had been agreed NO FOOD . . . Hunt had had his 'orrible dinner and I'd had toms/cheese/bread and was full . . . always happening. But it was light enough to eat with gusto. Nina has such dignity – partly the ballet dancer bearing but more than that. Fun watching Lorka and her have 'words' – reminiscent of me and Jake.

Flora came in at ten – only gone to *Pravda* bar and clearly not v. exciting after 1st flush of having a friend. Listened to Lorka's rock and roll. He's got a beaut old copy of *War and Peace* he's supposed to be reading for his school work – with his place marked by a Levi Strauss jeans label • • •

I was continually surprised by the breadth of Russian

magazines and newspapers, far more than I had imagined. *Pravda*, the Communist Party's official organ, is of course the biggest seller and the best known. You see it everywhere in Russia, most frequently in public lavatories, torn up neatly as lavatory paper. But it's not highly rated. *Izvestia* is thought slightly better, though there again it contains mainly official news, this time about the Soviets. The two best publications, according to my straw poll amongst writers and journalists, were *Sovietskaya Rossya* for news, and *Literaturnaya Gazeta*, for features. The latter does not just do books, despite its name, but covers a wide range of the arts, and also news stories, and is loved by the intellectuals. There's also a very popular youth publication called *Sobesednik*.

Russian newspapers and magazines might not be able to criticise the Party, but they do have great scope and freedom in exposing corruption, even amongst Party officials, hounding down local baddies and naming names.

Almost all those I spoke to poured scorn on the stories put out by dissidents, suggesting that we in the West had got it wrong, typical anti-Russian propaganda. I mentioned Irina Ratushinskaya, the poet said to be 'the best in Russia', but not one person had heard of her. I named other dissidents, well-known in the West, but they denied all knowledge of them. They did know the names of some people who had left, but they tended to be singers, musicians, artists, rather than writers. They talked fondly of them, people who had fallen foul of the system, and whom they now missed.

'Those writers you keep talking about, they were not published in Russia,' said one poet. 'So how would we know them? They make up a lot of their story, think up things they can sell to the Western press. It's obvious.'

'There are no political prisoners in Russia. They must have committed some crime against the state. Writing poetry is not enough. They must have taken part in demonstrations when they were warned not to, or distributed subversive literature.'

This was a line they all took, convinced of the fairness of the Russian legal system, though one or two admitted, privately, they had Jewish friends who had been hounded, unfairly forced out of their jobs for speaking out.

'I have a Jewish friend who has no job now. His friends in Israel send him parcels of food and clothes, which he sells on the black market, to keep himself alive. That's against the law, so the KGB are always raiding his flat, searching his car, looking for evidence.'

They felt personally free, able to express themselves, live their lives the way they wanted, give or take the usual moans about the economy and queues. All writers know what they can't write about, such as attacks on the government, and almost all agreed with that. They considered them sensible rules, for the good of their nation. I was of course meeting Writers' Union writers, those who wouldn't be there if they thought otherwise.

They felt genuinely sorry for us in the West, at the mercy of the capitalist rat race, forced to compete endlessly, with Money as the one great God, manipulated by international firms, bombarded by commercial advertising, pornography on every shelf, young people killing themselves with drugs. All true, of course. I'm sure most Russians are utterly shocked on their first visit to London.

This total lack of real envy for our way of life was a revelation. They might admire our jeans or pop music, T-shirts and motor cars, but that was about all. For the first time in my life I realised there would *not* be a mass exodus, if the barriers were ever down. Most Russians would stay. If only their short-sighted government would realise this, they could save themselves a lot of problems.

On the subject of Afghanistan, there was a totally different reaction. In this case, almost all admitted, rather sadly, that they did not approve of what their government had got themselves into. They had read what they had been told, that Russia had to do it, but they didn't believe it. It should never have been allowed. They had all heard privately of the loss of lives, mainly in peasant villages, miles away. The army has been careful not to send too many Muscovites, so the tales of the tragedies are not being re-told on their own doorstep.

I must have spoken in all to about thirty different people, and only one, a journalist called Yuri, was a hard-line defender of the government. It was justified, he said, because: a) we were invited in to help a legally installed government under threat from guerillas; b) you have to understand that Afghanistan is in the belly of Russia, right on our border, so we have to protect ourselves; c) Americans will set up missile sites there, just as they have done in Greece and Turkey, and anyway they are already supporting the rebels with money and arms. 'But we will withdraw as soon as we can. That is the aim. Only today, Gorbachev has announced six divisions are coming home.'

I asked why the Russian people were kept in the dark about the fighting. 'That is not true. Battles are reported, the ups and the downs. But why should we list casualties? It is a war. It would be bad for morale. Did Britain do that in the last war?'

It seemed to me a big diplomatic mistake. Russia had been winning the propaganda war, amongst the non-aligned countries, as a country which wants peace, more than the Americans. But now, with Afghanistan, they have ruined their image.

'That is because the true facts of the case have not been reported, just as I am sure the true facts about Britain ill-treating Catholic prisoners in Ulster have not been reported . . .'

M. • • • Flora has made another friend, or rather a friend made Flora – a rather beautiful girl we've been smiling at. Name unpronounceable as yet. She spoke to Flora, who was delighted, and suggested meeting at 3 pm and going to look round the Pravda House – what joy to have an arrangement of one's own, never mind what. We had our Georgian snack at lunch and toms., then F. toddled off.

I read and Hunt lolled, exhausted after talking to a journalist with v. poor Eng. (another friend he's made). Flora got a jellyfish stuck *inside* her cossie on her tum – I had to reach in and scrape it out – luckily didn't sting.

Two Afghanistan soldiers came down to swim – like Canadian Mounties in long boots and big hats, all dark green. They swam miles and miles out and when they got dressed put their long trousers straight over their long blue wet shorts. Various workmen came down to swim too and did the same. (F goes mad if Hunt calls them peasants.) • • •

Perhaps the most entertaining friend I made, who became a regular visitor to our little corner of the Solarium, was seventeen-year-old Fyodor, the Boy Wonder.

It was his mother who spoke to me first. She had heard my name mentioned, she said, and immediately went upstairs to her son and said guess who's staying here, from London, England. 'When I told him, he fell out of bed!'

One naturally feels softened up by such an approach, so I said fine, send him along some time, though I wondered if I had the energy left for someone else to practise their English on.

He was tall, rather ungainly, very young and gauche-looking, with total concentration and utter passion for whatever he was talking about – and the most incredible English. He started learning it at three, he said, and was

136

fluent at seven. 'Though my spelling was rather shaky.'

You can excuse such boasting, when you can see the evidence of it in the flesh. His father is a distinguished Russian academic and writer, Dimitri Urnov, a member of the Academy of Sciences and other notable bodies. 'You can say he is a man of letters and the author of fifteen books.' Because of his position, his father travels abroad quite often, to international conferences. When Fyodor heard his first Beatles record, aged ten, and became passionate about them, his father was able to help.

'My father is the sort of person who, when you ask him a question, does not reply, but says here are fifteen books on the subject, look it up, my boy.'

Fyodor was given first of all a Russian book called a *Dictionary of Modern Thought*, where he looked up the Beatles and found a reference to the 1968 authorised biography, written by a certain H. Davies. He asked his father to get it, which he did, during a visit to Japan, and then young Fyodor committed every page to memory.

Oh come on, I said. You're pulling my leg. Someone has put you up to this.

There and then, he started reciting page after page. I recognised bits, but couldn't remember half of it, as it took place such a long time ago.

After that, he got his father to buy other Beatles books, and very soon he was a legend in his lunchtime, at least in his school playground, as Moscow's youngest Beatleologist. On December 8, 1981, the first anniversary of John Lennon's death, he wore a black headband to school, but had to take it off as the teachers did not approve.

The sad thing was that I let him down so many times. I had to explain that, though I still love the Beatles dearly, I have written another twenty books since then, all on completely different topics, and now, in my middle years, the old memory is going. But he insisted on asking me what I *really* thought about Pete Shotton (Who? Oh yeh, that school friend of John's), and what Derek Taylor is doing these days (formerly the Beatle PR man) and is Aunt Mimi still alive (John's aunty, who brought him up).

'Tell me, sir, why did Paul do "Broad Street"? I sometimes despair of Paul. Why does he write such boring music these days? How can anyone do that who wrote "Eleanor Rigby", which is a work of genius. But I suppose it was always in him. Think of "Oobly Dee Oobly Da".'

Ah, hold on Fyodor, that was pastiche, a joke West Indian song. I *know* that, he said, just as I know what fish and finger pie is (a rather rude Liverpool expression) and that Lucy in the Sky was not LSD.

His English was full of slang, slightly out of date, going back to Sixties words like grotty, and at the same time he insisted on calling me sir, saying gee and I guess, like a well brought-up American youth. He could also do, which was remarkable, considering he had never met any English people before, a very good Liverpool accent.

He asked me about Yoko, what I thought when I first met her, how the rest of the Beatles had really reacted when she had come along. 'Can I give you my opinion, sir? And do you mind if I use a rude expression?' I wondered what was coming. Did he know English four-letter words as well? 'I think, sir, she is a silly bitch.'

I found him always amusing, but I suspect that others, particularly his contemporaries, were not so enthralled. Often, as we sat chatting, other boys like Lorka, or Lorka's school friends Stas and Constantine, would move away, knowing they'd never get a word in, not with Fyodor around. One adult, who was doing a drawing of Flora, actually told him to belt up, he was being a pain.

He was very proud of his English and very contemptuous of Russian kids walking around in T-shirts which said things like 'D'ya think I'm sexy?' or 'I love NY' without understanding the message. He usually wore a more sedate

USA T-shirt with a trolley on it which said 'San Francisco, California', brought back by his father.

I had assumed by his age he must still be at school, and that English must be his main subject, but he is a scientist, has already finished his first year at Moscow University where he is reading Biology. 'I want to discover how cells multiply. I would like to be the new Alexander Fleming. I'd also like to be a member of the Russian Academy of Science.' And a Nobel Prize? 'Yes that would be nice.' I said I'd keep my eye out for his name, on the list of future winners. And it was from then on that we called him the Boy Wonder, instead of just Beatle Brain.

One day on the Solarium we had a chat with him on Communism, though it did seem a bit unfair to cross-examine a seventeen-year-old, even a Boy Wonder, as most people's political views change with age and experience. He was a totally loyal Party member. He had enjoyed the Pioneers, which isn't really political, just good fun when you're young. But he also liked the Komsomol, the Young Communist League, which was not compulsory, but he was proud to be a member.

He admitted the usual faults in the economy, saying the Party was still working towards its goal. 'Elections are a farce, but they are getting better.' He saw no fault in the censorship system, which was a surprise, for someone of his age, interested in popular culture. 'I would not like to think of one tree being cut down so that bad words could be printed. I am against pornography. There is no excuse for it.' As for the other forms of censorship in the Russian press, he agreed with those as well. 'All our publishing companies are Government-owned. Would you expect them to allow anti-State propaganda? Of course not.

'In your Beatles book, sir, the first edition, you did not

139

mention Brian Epstein's homosexuality. You were censored. We have similar rules in Russia, which I agree with.'

I did once witness him getting something wrong, though I'd not noticed it myself. First thing one morning, he had arrived on the Solarium and said to us, 'How do you do?' His mother came up and told him off. 'In English,' she said, 'one says simply "Good morning" to someone you already know, not "How do you do?"'

Meanwhile, Flora's social life was becoming even busier. And not just on the teenage circuit, but amongst an even older crowd, from what we could observe in brief glimpses.

It was becoming hard to remember that first night at Pitsunda, when Margaret and I argued about imposing this awful place on her, worried that she would have no friends and be absolutely bored.

She was now out every evening, going round the bars, while I usually went for an evening walk somewhere, usually into Pitsunda, and in the afternoon she took tea with Fatima, or it might have been Fatsima, a sensational-looking girl, rather Mongolian in looks, who had become her latest and most constant friend.

I then discovered that, with all the excitement of her new friends, Flora had given up her diary. She had religiously kept it each day in Moscow, and in Pitsunda for the first few days, much to my pleasure. We'd all agreed to keep one. It would be an experience she would not forget, going into the heart of Russia at her age. I'd always made the older ones, Jake and Caitlin, keep holiday diaries and notebooks. You forget. Oh yes, you do. The little things just fade away. And it's the account of the little things, the details of the people you met, which brings all the big things back.

So I moaned at her to get back to her diary. After all, it sounded as if she had something decent to record, though of course I know that having something decent to do is much more fun than writing about it.

F. • • • It is now Friday and I have done hardly any of this pathetic diary, but Hunt is desperate for me to carry on as he has images of making his diary into a book and adding parts of mine and M's. That's the real reason. Bloody 'ell.

So I now may as well write it as a story, not as something personal, so daddy can find it pleasant to READ.

I am not going to write it as a blow by blow account of each day but just of interesting 'things'.

*FATSIMA – is a beautiful girl of 16 from Tashkent. I met her on the beach on Tuesday. She came to me and chatted in very good English (having been learning it since she was 8). We have spent the last 3 days partly together, at tea, on beach and going to the *Pravda* and Cinema House bars in the evening, and hanging around as the weather has been cloudy.

She is here with her mother and sister who is 9 and equally beautiful.

Fatsima has played lead roles in 2 films and at a film festival. In Italy, I think.

*HELEN I met while on the beach with F. Alex had told her I was English so they came and talked to us. She is 21 and is here on her honeymoon with her Russian husband who is a journalist. She's studying English at the Institute of Foreign Languages in Moscow, speaks very good English (especially compared to Alex who can only say 1 sentence and gets confused with that and has to make hand gestures).

She's very jolly and friendly and invited us to the *Pravda* bar that evening. We didn't realise how old they were: her husband was broad, beefy and smiled a lot though couldn't

141

speak English and sat with his flask of wine throughout. It was me, Helen and Hubby, Alex, Fatsima, 3 other blokes of about 19-25 and 2 girls whom I couldn't see quite clearly enough.

I AM NOT GOING TO WRITE ANY MORE ON THE SUBJECT AS 1) MY HAND IS TIRED 2) I CAN REMEMBER IT FOR MYSELF VERY WELL 3) IT IS NOT WORTH PUTTING IN A BORING BOOK.

*ALLI is a supposed friend of Fatsima's, though she says she hates him and he follows her everywhere. He is 18, tall, thin, very dark and I suppose good-looking, in a weird way. He lives in the same district of Tashkent as F and they did things together, before I arrived. F says because there was nothing else to do and he was the only person she knew. She says he is thick, 'immodest' and annoying • • •

CHAPTER ELEVEN

Excursions and Alarms

Originally, we had no intention of going on any outings, after all those rather tiring tours and expeditions in Moscow, but the poor weather returned, humid and cloudy, and we began to feel we would perhaps like a slight change from our Solarium routine.

Our first little expedition was our own doing. I suggested that we spend a morning in Gagra, the nearest town, about twenty miles away along the coast. We'd passed it on the journey from the airport and it looked nice. There was supposed to be a much bigger market there, so we could stock up on vegetables and fruit, perhaps find some new stuff.

I told Sasha, our supposed Minder, that we were going to catch the local bus at the end of the road, and he twittered on, saying would I be able to cope, what if I got lost, did he want me to come with him, I said no problem, old sport. We've got bags of money left. If we get stuck, we can get a taxi back.

Flora said she would come, jolly good of her, as I presumed she would prefer to be with her new friends, but I think she too fancied a change, and anyway the

weather was a bit poor for sunbathing. I invited Fatsima
to come as well, thinking I'd done the right thing, but
Flora said I should not have done. I should not interfere.
If she wanted to invite her friends, that was up to her. I
also invited Lorka. Listen, Flora, he's now *my* friend, as
you don't appear interested in him. I can invite anyone I
like, so there.

So the five of us set off, me and Margaret, plus the
three teenagers. I saw Lorka not just as my chum but my
translator, even though he didn't speak Georgian or know
the area any more we did.

We stood in a bus shelter, and I insisted on taking
Lorka's photograph. Flora refused, as she always does
when I ask her, rotten thing. It was an amazing shelter,
about the size of two double-deckers, shaped like an
Octopus, decorated with different-coloured bits of tiles,
like a mosaic. I'd noticed a few of these along the road, all
in mad shapes and forms, animals and fish, rather crude in
a way, amateur art, but very individual and idiosyncratic,
not the sort of daft thing you'd expect in a people's
republic, where design tends to be so standardised.

We were joined in the bus shelter by some other people
from the hotel, who'd also decided to go to Gagra. One of
them was a friend Margaret had made, a ship's doctor
who wrote adventure stories. She thought he had excellent
English at first, till we realised he always prepared just
two or three sentences, very fluently, and would wander
up and declaim them like an actor, smile at his own wit,
then wander off. If you followed up anything, or asked
him a question, he was lost, unable to say anything else,
until he prepared his next speech. But he was helpful, and
told us which bus to get, and where to get off. He was
going to Gagra simply to make a phone call home to
Leningrad. He'd failed to get anywhere with the hotel
switchboard.

M. • • • When the bus did arrive, it was absolutely packed, but that's never any obstacle – they never refuse anyone. We all pressed into a completely crowded bus and even then at the next stop they let more on. There was an extremely fierce fat lady taking the money. Journey took 25 minutes, strap-hanging and squashed all the way. Great indecision at the bus station in Gagra: where was the market? The ship's doctor (whom we called AJ Cronin) pointed in one direction for the market, but then some locals pointed in the other and an old woman sd. we'd need a bus. . . . First we set off in one direction, then another with poor Lorka valiantly asking the way. He and the girls wanted to get a taxi but H was against. In the end, we walked and asked people along the way. Half the route was a busy road but the other a track leading past quite pretty houses with gardens and vines everywhere. The market was unattractive – a big concrete hall, 2 tier, in a big concrete square, mountains to the right (v. Lake District) and new flats round the rest. Huge piles of water melons everywhere and sinister-looking men behind them. One, in a leather waistcoat, black hair and moustache, swarthy and evil-looking, stuck a wicked-looking knife into melons to cut them and show they were good and I felt a flutter of alarm just watching him – so easy to imagine the knife used for other purposes. All the faces behind the stalls were fascinating – much darker and more rugged than any we've seen before. It was mainly melons, toms, peppers, a few aubergines and of course pots of yoghurt and lots of goat's cheese • • •

Flora and Fatsima said they wanted to go off and explore the market on their own. They'd seen some interesting-looking jewellery and clothes stalls on the far side. So we made a rendezvous for half an hour's time. After forty

145

minutes, they hadn't turned up and we were becoming worried.

Lorka stood with us, his young eyes scanning the crowds. 'You should not have let them go,' he said very solemnly. 'These Georgians are hot-blooded . . .' He shook his head like an old woman. We laughed, but the longer they were away, the more we became slightly concerned. I had noticed one very dodgy-looking Georgian youth on the bus, who had been pressing himself against Fatsima and muttering things in her ear.

They suddenly appeared from another direction, arm in arm, chattering and smiling, working their way through the throng. They were carrying three ice-creams and had a long story about the huge queue for them. Flora was very pleased with herself – having been thoughtful enough to bring one for Lorka. She was also holding a packet of hair grips which she said Fatsima had insisted on buying for her. 'A leetle present for a visitor.'

There was a sudden rain storm, so we decided we had better head back. Lorka wanted to get a taxi, but I'd noticed a little local bus, beat-up and old-fashioned. 'I travel in such inhuman conditions every day to school,' he said with disgust. I dunno. These spoiled, middle-class urban children are everywhere.

I asked an old woman if the bus was going to the main bus station, and she appeared to say yes, so I shepherded my gang on board, then I asked Lorka to check with the driver, ask him where he was going. 'Oh, I don't know where I'm going,' he replied to Lorka. Quite a joker.

He had some football team photographs pasted up around him in his cabin, and three pathetic pin-ups. They were just the faces of some pretty girls, cut out of some magazine, totally chaste, from the neck up. I thought of what he would have cut out if he lived in the disgusting, decadent West.

146

M. • • • We did our one and only proper expedition today, a whole day out to a town called Novi Afon to see some caves, along with 30 or so other people from the hotel, including Sasha and his family, Lorka and Nina. Flora refused to come. She couldn't think of anything more boring than sightseeing in the hills.

It was a perfect morning and the coach ride wasn't as long or agonising as we'd feared and it *was* interesting to see some of the countryside. We went south this time, through magnificently lush country, thickly wooded hills with the gt. blue peaks of the Caucasus behind – like a combination of the Lake District and Tuscany. The guide (who kept up a guttural commentary all the way, translated in a whisper by Sasha) was keen to point out the collective farms (producing tobacco, etc.) and to extol the virtues of the revolution which had reclaimed this malaria-infested swamp and made it as we saw. Noticed several rather beautiful houses, French château-style, washed in pink or apricot and lots of smaller houses in a similar shape. The cows were a pale tawny colour and there were several thoroughbred-looking horses galloping about – all of it 100 times more lovely than Pits.

At Novi Afon we parked the bus at a park and all got out and were led thro' it by our guide at a Russian trudge – v. boring. He stopped at every flower bed and statue and gave a lecture – yawn, yawn – but then we began to climb to an old monastery that was brilliant – a fortress sort of shape with domes and all of it a pinky/apricot sun-bleached/rain-washed colour. There was a courtyard in the middle, cobbled, with trees here and there. I sat and watched the other tourists after a quick look inside – painted frescoes in a cavern-like musty neglected sort of church. Very hot by now. The other defector from our party was the Turkish poet. His younger daughter almost had a nasty accident – ran with a bottle in her hand and fell and the broken neck of it just missed her own neck.

147

Cut down to another park thro' which a stream ran with a waterfall at one end. Dreadful packed lunch but we bought some tomatoes. Then we walked with Lorka and Nina to the top of the waterfall where, a little way on, there was a splendid railway station. It lay between two tunnels and was beautifully painted – lots of black and white wrought iron work. Hunt was just getting ice-cream and coffee when a train came and he yelled at me to get the camera and take him against the train. I dutifully rushed and had just clicked the shutter when Sasha arrived greatly agitated – 'You'd better be careful, no photographs are allowed.' There were signs everywhere to that effect. I noticed for the first time that the man in the signal box had a rifle. We apologised profusely, but there was one of those slight atmospheres that are so strange. The Russians are embarrassed by the rules, but also defiant – they don't want them mocked or scorned and are content to believe them necessary.

Long trudge up to the entrance to the famous caves we were going to see – by now baking hot. Not much enthusiasm for seeing it except it would be cold. We went into the bowels of the mountain in a little train and then walked along a specially constructed path with handrails either side. It was an extraordinary journey of about a mile, I think – up and down and over and through these gigantic caves with sinister underground pools in the depths of them. As a feat of engineering it was remarkable – cunning lights illuminating stalagmites and -tites – and as an accident of nature it was phenomenal.

They played spooky music as we slowly followed the trail and, as I looked ahead at the silent, shuffling people slowly trudging on, it made me think of tired prisoners in a salt mine. There were six caves, all connected, and at each we stopped and were told millions of facts. The light was dim with spotlights focused on special bits and this sent great frightening shadows everywhere. It was cool but not the bitter cold we'd expected. In the last cave, to demonstrate the perfect acoustics, they played Bach. The record went slightly wonky which disturbed the reverential hush.

A woman, young but fat, trudged all thro' the caves carrying a 2 yr. old. Her image – patient, stoical, *apparently* impervious to either the weight of the child or the beauty of the caves – seemed v. Russian.

Back to the bus and an easy ride home with more vistas of hills and rolling wooded country. Only the new modern constructions like our Writers' House defile the landscape. It gets harder and harder to understand why, with all this land, they build these high-rise monstrosities.

Flora off to the *Pravda* bar – I slumped, exhausted. Hunt braved supper. I was hungry but only for something delicious, attractively presented – nothing would drive me into that dining room and those trolleys of disgusting slop • • •

We did have one meal out, during our stay in Pitsunda. Nina and Lorka, plus me, Margaret and Flora, decided to try dinner in a Georgian restaurant that someone had recommended. Sasha was a bit worried when he heard we were going. He said the meat would be hot, we wouldn't like it, it would be dangerous to eat, and the Georgians would cheat us.

I was very pleased to discover it had live music, a four piece group, with a very good girl singer. We started with a herb pâté, which was strong and spicy. Margaret had trout for her main course. Flora had nothing, being a vegetarian and not fancying anything. Lorka and I had meat, great huge kebab-like chunks of it. I thought it was terrific, though they gave us too much. Margaret thought it looked revolting.

There was no problem about wine, even though it was

well after seven o'clock. We got through two bottles. Well, I did. It was local Georgian wine, which tasted faintly like Retsina.

It was a very jolly meal, conducted mainly in English and French, as Nina prefers to speak French with us. Lorka was wearing yet another T-shirt which proclaimed 'People's March for Freedom, 1982'. It had been bought for him in Britain by his father.

We ate outside, but towards the end, when it was getting dark, we moved to a table inside, near the music. They were playing what sounded like a folk song, but with a rock and roll backing rhythm. I was sure I could hear the word 'Brighton' in the chorus, though the rest of the song was totally in Russian. I told Lorka and Nina to listen carefully, in case my ears were playing tricks, and translate it.

'Today we're in Brighton,
Tomorrow on Broadway,
Goodbye to Moscow.'

It was obviously a dissident song, about someone who had managed to escape to England. Nina looked worried and said I should not write down the words, not there and then. The singers might become alarmed.

I walked into Pitsunda on my own one night, to get some wine, and I was stopped by several people, newly arrived tourists, who asked in Russian where the wine shop was. I was able to point them in the right direction, indicating I was going that way. I soon had quite a queue of people following me. The Pied Piper of Pitsunda.

Two well-built youths aged about twenty, both in rather natty sports clothes, carrying tennis rackets and a large old-fashioned tape recorder, started talking to me. They'd never met an English person before and had forgotten

150

most of what they had learned at school. They were both at Moscow University, studying physics, now on holiday at a summer camp for students. I'd noticed quite a few such places, wooden chalets, with communal washrooms, behind a high fence. I said the huts looked a bit basic, like youth hostels, but they said no, it was great. 'We have a bed each, food, the sun, and girls. And it's only one rouble a week. What more do we want?'

Wine, I suggested. They both smiled. That was what they now hoped to get, if I would lead them to the wine shop.

'You don't see any drunks in the streets now, not the way you used to,' said one of them. I admitted I hadn't seen one since coming to Russia. The nearest was in Pitsunda when I saw a local bloke being helped into a taxi, singing. But the rich can still manage it, I said, if they are willing to buy drinks on the black market. 'Oh yes, and real drunks will still queue all day for vodka, but there's no hope for them anyway. What the new rules do is stop young people starting to drink. That was the real problem. That was very bad for our country. The results so far have been very good. There are twenty per cent fewer deaths from drunken driving now.'

'If Lenin were alive,' said the other, 'things would have gone even faster.'

I thought at first he'd said Stalin and I told them about an amazing sight I'd seen that day at our hotel, in the queue for the Hachipuree. I was in my bathing costume, as most people were, but I thought at first the young man beside me was in a T-shirt, which displayed on it the smiling face of Stalin. I then realised the man was bare-chested. The face of Stalin was a tattoo. I think he might have been a local workman, as I'd never seen him before. I tried all afternoon without success to find him again. I wanted to take his photograph.

The boys listened and said they were not surprised. The

151

rest of the Soviet Union did think Stalin had been a bad man, and he was not referred to in history books any more, but there were people in his homeland of Georgia who believed he had been a very good leader, despite his faults, who had won the war for Russia.

They wanted to know about unemployment in England, not to criticise or score points, but to understand it. What happens to people who are unemployed, what do they do? I explained that the Government gave them money, so that no one actually starved. They stopped and stared at this, unable to believe it. When I told them how much, they were truly astounded. 'If I was in England, I would like to be unemployed,' said one with a laugh.

I explained that the money did not go as far as it would in Russia, though we did have free national health and subsidised council houses, just as they did in Russia. They stopped and stared again. It was the free health that had particularly surprised them. They had assumed England was like America, a totally capitalist country.

I said Britain had had several Socialist Governments, and would again soon. They must not judge us all by Mrs Thatcher. They rather admired her, they said, even though she was right wing. They thought most people in Russia did. The Russian taunt about her being the 'Iron Lady' was not meant as a sneer, but out of admiration. She was the sort of leader they could understand. 'Russians like strong leadership.'

It was interesting to talk to 'ordinary' young Russians, whose only knowledge of the West was picked up from the Russian press, or rumours. In the Writers' Hotel, many of the writers had either been to the West, or had access to our press, so they knew a surprising amount. The latest rumour they'd heard was that Gorbachev had arrived, yes, truly, here in Pitsunda, hadn't I seen the helicopters and the warship? The Party has a dacha, they said, just the other side of the town. I had to look out for it, though I wouldn't be able to get near. He was here for his summer holidays.

Last year, when they were in Pitsunda, they'd been told that our Mr Scargill had been here. What happened to that strike? Did the miners win? I expected they would be sorry for Scargill, as we in Britain were led to believe he was a hero in Russian eyes. But no. They approved of the British Government having won. 'It's not right that people should go on strike. People should do what their Government directs.'

I looked at them, these two modern youths, a chance meeting, who looked so familiar in their clothes and styles, yet so different in their basic attitudes. You can get young people in Britain who are against the miners, and against strikes, but believing that a government should always be obeyed would surprise most young people in the West.

'The thing I envy about the West,' said one, 'is the cars. I know, when I get a job, I'll only get 200 roubles a month. A car in Russia costs 7,000, so I'll never manage that.'

We reached the wine shop with only fifteen minutes to go before closing time at seven. I wanted two bottles, which was what I'd got last time, but I was only allowed one for some reason.

When we got out, one of the boys presented me with his bottle. I said no, no, you need both your bottles, it wouldn't be fair. I'll survive, it's just greed anyway.

No, we want you to have it. Please take it. In that case, I said, I must pay you. But they wouldn't accept any money. I had become embarrassed. Two students, hard up, living cheaply, and there they were, giving me a bottle of their wine, their ration, which cost two roubles, a lot for them.

'It is a custom in Russia to always give a stranger something to drink. So this is our gift.'

We walked all the way to the bus station together, still chattering, with me wondering how I could repay their

153

kindness. They got on the same bus as me, as they were going to have a game at the tennis court in the *Pravda* grounds.

After I'd shaken hands, and said goodbye, I raced up to our room and got out two of my *Beatles Monthlies*, then I went to find them at the *Pravda*.

They were sitting waiting their turn for the court, while two wizened ladies were playing, looking rather furious. My two friends had got out their tape-recorder and placed it on the seat between them. They'd put on 'Dire Straits' and were playing it full blast. I made my little presentation and shook hands again. I could still hear their music blaring out, all the way back to the Writers' building.

F. • • • There is a girl of about 16 who sits at the next table with 2 sisters and father. She is very striking, but I don't know about 'pretty'. I would like to talk, but I don't know enough Russian and I get no response when I smile at her, though dad's friend Vladimir said that Russians 'Smile in their heads'. So dad said. Well that's no bloody use then, is it.

Went to Pravda at 9 and met a Georgian girl of about 19 called Tatzia who has long frizzy hair and looked beautiful, though not so much if you really study her. She has huge almond eyes and looks quite Italian. She sat and said 'yes I find it dull'.

Nina, another Georgian girl, was going to draw a portrait of mum, having studied art for 7 years. She now wants to draw *moi*!

Alex sat for 2 hours asking me if I liked Freddy Mercury and Queen, saying he was his hero and then asking, 'What do you think about the health of your Queen?! And Mrs Thatcher?' Alex is the ugliest most unattractive 'guy', but is funny and willing, OK yar.

Later went to the Barbecue. All day Lorka and Stas and Constantinou had repeatedly asked excitedly if me and F

154

were coming. They spent the whole morning 'fishing' for mussels. They appeared with two huge plastic bags full of them, but were a little disgruntled because, according to them, people were scared that they were radio-active. I had trouble in eating any and hid them under the pebbles on the beach • • •

CHAPTER TWELVE

Black Sea Barbecue

It was through Flora we first heard about the beach barbecues. While I had been having my evening walk, usually on my own, and her Mama had been sitting sedately reading on our balcony, Flora had not only been going round the bars with all these older girls and boys, but ending up afterwards on the beach, having good times in the dark. No wonder she had been so late recently.

I suppose I should have guessed that all was not as it seemed. In the dining room, the families looked so staid and proper, bowing and bending to each other, all apparently going up to their rooms at a respectably early hour. With all these teenagers around, I might have known there would be something happening, somewhere. Russians are human. Wild orgies on the beach? Drunken swimming parties? Not quite.

It was thanks to Albert, a writer of children's books, that I was invited to my first barbecue, after we had been out fishing one day.

We went out in two little rowing boats. Me and Albert in one. Stas and Con, Lorka's two school friends, in the other. I don't know much about fishing, but it did seem strange when Albert gave me a rod with ten hooks on it. It was very hard to hold, without getting it all tangled. There was no bait on any of the hooks, so I waited for him to put some on, but he said it wasn't necessary. 'Must be pretty stupid fish,' I said, 'if you can catch them with a bare hook.' 'Yes,' he said. 'They're Georgian fish.'

Albert's English was poor, which was a shame, as I felt he was keen to tell me lots of things. 'So many things wrong with our country,' he said. 'I feel happiest when I fish.' He then concentrated on telling me what to do, the places to drop my line, how to let it sink right to the seabed, wait for a tickle, then pull it in, keeping it always dead straight. Several times he had to take over my rod and unwind all the hooks, as I'd got them in such a mess.

We had a competition with the other boat, to see who could catch most, shouting out the totals so far. I could manage that, at least up to twenty, which is as far as my Russian numerals can go. We were fishing for Stavrida, a Black Sea form of sardine, quite small, but very satisfying to catch. My best was three, all in one go. We got twenty-four altogether in our boat. Albert was a bit disappointed. On a good day, he has caught over a hundred Stavrida. Seven on one rod is his record.

I did think I'd caught at least ten on my rod when there was a sudden gigantic weight on my line. My arms ached with the struggle to pull it in, but I managed it. It turned out to be a shark. It threw itself around the bottom of the boat, in a great fury, lashing with its fins. I could see its jaw quite clearly, so I kept my bare legs well out of the way while Albert stunned it. It was probably only three feet long, but it did look enormous when it first came into the boat. It got smaller and smaller as the morning went on, as it lay on the bottom, shrinking in the midday sun.

It really was a shark. No kidding. The Boy Wonder confirmed it, and he is reading biology. It was a Catran, a special Black Sea shark, though just a young one. When

157

fully grown, they are only two metres, not as big or as fierce as a Pacific shark, but of the same family.

Naturally, I boasted like mad to Margaret and Flora, and ran around telling everyone, saying I was going to eat it that evening. Albert had invited the three of us to his beach barbecue. Wow. I'd secured an invitation at last. Sucks to you, Flora Davies.

M. • • • As near to a clear day as we've had – authentic blue sky, no cloud at all, strong sun – but the air is still somehow v. slightly hazy and humid, tho' on the sun deck there's a lovely breeze. Spent all morning there, not even reading. Hunt went fishing.

Talked to Galina, an interpreter who goes back and forwards to GB – brill English, had been to Brighton last yr. She actually seemed to think this was 'a lovely spot' – must be mad – and 'just like Brighton'. What a puzzle. But all criticism is hurtful – except of the food. They all agree about the food being terrible – Galina says they have endless complaints and meetings about it.

A Georgian girl called Nina came to talk to me – to say how the *Pravda* bar was electrified by Flora and then to ask if she could draw my portrait tomorrow. Hunt's *Pravda* friend Vladimir also came to talk but oh the strain of understanding his English, esp. as he wants to say such complicated things. In fact, in general the strain is exhausting – how much I depend on *talk* to make my way. I know it's a strain for them too, even more so. Surprising we've got as far as we have in communicating, considering the odds against.

Hunt returned from fishing and claimed he'd caught a baby shark. When I saw it later it was indeed a baby – must have been born that morning by the pathetic size of it. More like a large tadpole • • •

F. • • • Hunt came back thrilled with himself because they had caught a baby shark. (Oh my Gawd, I'll never go in the water again.) • • •

There wasn't just one barbecue that night, but several going on, right along the beach. It was a most attractive sight, the lights and the sounds from the little groups of people drinking and enjoying themselves. It was illegal, so I was told. A beach is a public place, and drinking alcohol in a public place is now not allowed.

We were having an all-fish barbecue, but further away I could smell meat. A few days previously I had got into the lift one evening and found drops of blood on the floor. Very alarming. I later noticed two youths carrying a rather nasty-looking bundle, wrapped in newspapers. It must have been raw meat, taking it to the beach, but at the time I didn't know about the all-night barbecues.

M. • • • There were two fires going at our barbecue. Lorka and Stas presided over one – they had a piece of corrugated iron over it and were cooking mussels on the iron. Considering where they got them – in a v. dirty-looking bit of sea near what looked suspiciously like a sewage pipe – we didn't want to eat them, but they were so thrilled at doing them a good show had to be put on. On the other fire, fish like small sardines were cooked in a covered pan and they were delicious. It was nice sitting round the fire at the edge of the sea – v. relaxed, no heartiness.

Stas's father is a famous crime writer – lovely jovial bearded fat man. His 2 younger children are exceptional in smiling all the time – gives the lie to theories about Russian dourness • • •

159

As the evening warmed up, the wine flowed and the talk got freer, people came and went, moving between groups, bringing friends back and forward.

I got introduced to a famous stage director from Moscow, who'd had a play on at the National Theatre in London. Everybody was most impressed by him as he produces classic Russian plays, as well as modern things with rock and roll music. He sounded like a Russian version of Trevor Nunn. His name was Mark Rozovsky. He later gave me a signed copy of one of his plays. He spoke no English, which was a shame.

I also met a playwright from Kiev, Jaroslav Stelmack, who asked me what I knew about Dale Wasserman. He was translating his play *One Flew Over the Cuckoo's Nest* into Russian and was desperate for any information about him. I didn't know a thing. He had had twelve of his own plays put on, in Kiev, and also written five children's books. He'd been at home in Kiev when the Chernobyl disaster had happened. He remembers a rotten headache all day, and feeling a bit sick, but that was all. He writes in Ukrainian, not Russian, so his income always depends on being translated.

In talking to a dozen or so writers, wandering round the barbecues, I realised for the first time that success for the provincial ones, from the other Republics of the Soviet Union, means getting into Russian. You can make a living, writing in your own language, but it can be hard. On the other hand, if you do get a cheque from a far-flung republic, because your play or novel has been done on local radio out in the wilds, the chances are that you won't have to declare it for tax reasons. No one will ever find out you ever got it.

They all agreed that successful writers, along with composers and artists, are pretty well off, but the really big earners in the Soviet Union are the lorry drivers in Siberia. They are said to get 2,000 roubles a month, and worth every kopek, for putting up with Siberia. Some coal miners and nuclear power station workers also get well paid, around 500 a month.

Perhaps it was the dark, or the wine, but I seemed to hear quite a lot about money and wealth. They all knew people, not necessarily writers, who had little fortunes stashed away, all of it earned legally. Quite a few admitted to having £20,000 and more, in the State Bank. The Government is now concerned at savings just being idly accumulated. The reason is simple. There's so little to spend it on. Once you've bought your flat, your dacha, your car, and your children have left home, that's it. Living is so cheap, with hardly anything to pay for tax, heating, transport, entertainment. Foreign holidays are impossible, apart from places like Bulgaria or Hungary, so that's where they all go, and spend wildly on consumer goods.

They all knew about black market dealers, but for the successful middle classes there's no need for that sort of unpatriotic thing. They oil the system by judicious swapping, doing favours for people, passing on foreign goods, treating teachers who might give extra lessons to their less gifted children, helping to get them into the better Moscow Institutes.

I also heard stories of teenagers having drinking parties when their parents were away at the dacha, inviting in their friends and wrecking the place. Oh, just like the West. I heard Khrushchev referred to as a peasant, such a vulgar fellow, and a long saga about Brezhnev and alleged corruption involving his family. I didn't hear anything against Gorbachev. They all seem to think it's a refreshing change to have a civilised person at the helm.

I was told a very long joke about Gorbachev and Reagan. After the last summit meeting, they decided to swap secretaries for a year, all in the cause of East-West good relations. After a few months, the American secretary writes home from Moscow to say that she's enjoying it, but Mr Gorbachev insists that she wears a maxi skirt in the office. The Russian secretary writes home from Washington to say that she too is enjoying the swap, but that Mr Reagan wants her to wear a mini skirt in the office. 'I can't do that, of course. If I do, he'll see my gun, and my balls . . .'

It was at the barbecue, walking along the beach, that I met the first writer who openly complained about the lack of freedom. Everybody else had maintained they did not feel constricted in their work.

I think he had deliberately chosen the dark, and the two of us walking alone, to unload himself. 'If life is a circle, I am only living twenty-five per cent of it. I can't write the things I really want to write.' He therefore stuck to safe, non-fiction stuff, but he had finished a novel, which he kept in a drawer. 'I think many Russian writers have a novel in their drawer, waiting for things to change, so that it can be published. Probably after their death.'

He pointed out to sea and I thought he was struggling to form some complicated metaphor, then he pretended to be a frog man, splashing in the water. 'Look out for the marines. They'll be listening to me underwater . . .'

His English was not good enough to cross-examine him very closely, and he dropped the subject when we got back to the others. He produced a bottle of red Georgian wine, the first I'd seen, which was delicious. He'd got it under the counter, from a peasant farmer, miles inland. I asked him to give me instructions, and draw a map on a piece of paper.

The barbecue finished about eleven, quite respectable. Nobody was drunk. Only one person went for a swim afterwards from our party, and that was me. There was no sign of Flora all evening.

162

F. • • • Went to Cinema House bar which was almost empty but is much more aesthetic than *Pravda*. Sat on the roof looking across the sea at the sunset. Walked back on road because when I suggested the beach Fatsima said – 'no, no, we must not, because . . . it's wild . . . no, 'cos there are . . . NUDISTS! . . .' I laughed out loud, having thought she was going to say wild lions, or Georgian terrorists, but her face was quite serious.

Went into *Pravda* as Alex, Vasser, Ivana, etc were just going out, so we went to the pier with them where they all sat smoking and drinking vodka and laughing affectedly. It was just like being at a pub with Jake (not that I have been to a pub with Jake).

Fatsima was getting agitated so we left, but it was all in the best possible taste • • •

CHAPTER THIRTEEN

Farewell, Pitsunda

Flora and Margaret said I must be potty. It was an absolutely stupid expedition. It would lead to trouble, or I would get lost and be back late, and miss the talk which I had promised to give. The notice had already gone up in the hall of the hotel. 'H. Davies, English, tonight at 6.30.'

It was our last evening in Pitsunda and it was going to be very busy. Apart from my talk, I had invited a few friends to have a final farewell drink with us afterwards on the Solarium. The only trouble was I had no drink, at least not enough for all the people I had invited.

So I had decided to try and get some of the illegal wine, if I could find the farmhouse I'd been told about. Margaret refused to come of course, and Flora had more exciting things to do, so I talked Lorka into coming with me, as my guide and translator.

Lorka and I caught a local bus going into Pitsunda. Then we got another one which went miles up into the hills. We got off at the stop I think I'd been told to get off at, and the bus sped away in a cloud of dust. We stood at some crossroads, with me trying to remember the next instruction. Was it left or right? I saw a woman coming towards us and I said to Lorka, quick, ask her where the farmhouse is that sells wine. He began to look a bit nervous. I don't think he'd really understood me when I said I had a secret expedition I wanted him to come on. Just some silly English phrase.

No use asking a woman, he said. Women don't know such things, because they don't drink.

On your bike, I said, wondering what the Russian was for on your bike. You should see our women. My sister, social worker of our parish, she takes a few, I said. And my dear lady wife, till she came to this dotty country of yours with your dotty regulations, you should see her when she gets going. Just ask Flora.

Then we saw an old man coming towards us and I said go on, try him, look at that conk, I bet he's been to a few illegal stills.

'You know it is illegal,' said the old man, his breath sweet with some local potion. 'You know the penalties. People are too scared to sell it to you.'

That's it, said Lorka, it's no good, let's go home, and he turned in the direction of the bus stop. Oh, come on. We didn't win the war that way, giving up at the first hurdle, I mean *you* didn't win the war that way. I still had to keep remembering that, according to the Russians, they beat Hitler. History is so confusing. In America you've got to remember that the war didn't begin till they came in.

I saw another old man, coming from another direction, and I said ask him, this is the last attempt, then we'll give up.

'You know it is illegal,' said this bloke. 'You know the penalties. People are too scared to sell it to you.' Then there was a pause. 'Follow me.'

We walked in silence for about a mile and I kept on nudging Lorka to ask him what he meant, was it a joke, a trick, or had he just misunderstood? He eventually stopped at a cart track, up in the wild stuff, with little kids running

165

naked and cows all over the dirt track. He pointed to a farmhouse in the distance and said see that gate, the green one. Well, go round the side, not the front, and whatever you do, don't say I sent you.

We got to the green gate, as directed, then carefully went round the side of the farmhouse, and what a fright we got. As we turned the corner, two monster wild pigs came tearing at us. I don't suppose they were really wild, just allowed to roam free in the lanes, but they'd got it into their heads to guard the side-door. They were huge, with great long legs, not like our podgy British piggies.

We ran back the way we'd come, then stopped and eyed them as they grunted round our legs. Lorka spoke to them in Russian, he'd turned out useful after all, and we slowly made our way to the gate again, with the pigs escorting us. It was a modern metal gate, high and well-barricaded, rather out of character for a remote farm-house. As we stood wondering what to do next, we saw an old man come out of the farm door and hobble towards us.

Lorka explained I was an English visitor, very keen to sample the famous Georgian wines, and could he just see his way to letting us have a bottle? Three roubles, said the man, showing no expression. I gave him six roubles, passed my Heathrow Duty Free plastic bag through the gateway, and off he toddled.

The two pigs grunted all the time he was away. One of them had started to chew my Marks and Spencer trainers, my best pair, which had been nearly white when we'd started our expedition. A little girl came out of the farmhouse and watched us carefully. Lorka smiled and asked if they were her pigs, but she said nothing and went back inside.

The old feller seemed to have disappeared completely with my six roubles, and my plastic bag. He was probably on the phone to the police. The little girl had no doubt secretly taken photos of us. Both pigs were KGB officers in disguise.

He came back at last, trudging across the farmyard, and handed my bottles through the gate. I took them and we both ran off, as quickly as possible. I paused after a few hundred yards, to look inside, and see that the empty bottles I'd given him were full, and that he'd put the little plastic caps on.

There was a big queue for the bus home, locals having crawled out of what had seemed an uninhabited hillside. As we sat on a bench, waiting, there was a loud pop, then another. I could feel wine trickling down my legs. The smell was very strong and people were looking at us, muttering to each other in Georgian, then smiling and nodding their heads.

On the bus, I held the plastic bag securely between my knees, to avoid any more spillage, feeling pretty chuffed. I'll be able to give decent wine at my drinks tonight. And I won't give Margaret any. She can get her own. We had to struggle with wild boars to get these bottles, didn't we, Lorka?

I could sense some people on the bus staring at me, but then as a foreigner I'd got used to that. I discovered the reason when I got back to our hotel. The wine was so sour it was undrinkable. In fact I think it *was* vinegar that old feller had sold me.

Oh, how they roared and laughed. That will larn you, Hunt, it's a judgement on you, forcing poor Lorka to break the law with you, you deserve it, you greedy pig.

My talk was to take place in the cinema, not in the library as first planned, which was very flattering, as the cinema is the largest hall in the Writers' Home. And the subject was going to be the Beatles, what else, by popular request. OK, I had suggested it, offering my services to Sasha over a week previously, when I realised the great interest in the Fab Four. I wanted to give something back, a thank you, as they had all been so kind to us.

167

I had brought with me only one Beatles cassette from London, putting it in Flora's bag at the last moment, thinking I might borrow her Walkman some time, if things got boring. Fortunately, Lorka had with him a very good cassette player on which he was always playing his own tapes, copied from Western L.P.s. I'd noticed in his room his neat pile of cassettes, one of them marked 'Best of Rock and Rolls'.

Lorka said that he would be in charge of the music and, at an agreed signal, he would put on each number. I planned to begin the talk with a quiz, promising prizes for the winners – three copies of *Beatles Monthly*. I'd got five simple questions to ask the audience. 1) Name the four Beatles. 2) Which town in England did they come from? 3) Name a Beatle song. 4) When the Beatles split up, Paul began his own group. What was its name? 5) In which city did John Lennon die?

Fyodor, the Boy Wonder, thought the questions were infantile, and everyone would get them, but Sasha thought they were impossible, and few people would understand them. The more I talked to Sasha, the more I realised he didn't know much about the Beatles, yet he was going to do all the translating. I delicately suggested that perhaps it might be best if he just introduced me, as a sort of Master of Ceremonies, while Fyodor could do the actual translating of my speech. I worried that he might be upset, having his place taken by a seventeen-year-old boy, but he readily agreed.

It was an incredibly hot and sticky evening and, though all the doors of the cinema were left open, everyone was soon perspiring. But there was still an excellent audience. The cinema was full, which meant about 200 turned up.

I noticed that, for the first half-hour, Fyodor's translation of my English was taking twice as long in Russian. Russian is not a 'long' language, unlike German, where a translation can take up much more space. Then I realised, by picking out odd phrases, that he was putting in extra explanations and information, showing off his own knowledge, brilliant though it was. At this rate, we'd never get through my speech before dinner. So, when Lorka was playing a song to illustrate one of my points, I whispered to Fyodor to cool it, man, just to stick to my words, son.

While I talked, and Fyodor translated, and Lorka did the cassette player, Sasha was given the boring job of analysing the quiz answers. I wanted the all-correct answers in one pile, and also a list of the most mentioned song titles, for my own interest.

At the end of my speech, someone asked if it was true the Beatles had stopped off in Moscow, en route to Japan, and that was when they had written 'Back in the USSR'. I had to tell them this was only a legend. Another person asked if it was true, as the Russian press had just reported, that the three remaining Beatles were going to do a live concert, along with Julian Lennon. I said that was news to me. Perhaps they might, for charity, but I was sure they would never get together again as a group.

There were six all-correct answers to the quiz. I put them in a hat and looked round for a suitable person to pick out the winner. I thought of asking the prettiest girl, as they do on TV shows, but that might be considered by Flora as being sexist. I wasn't sure if she was in the audience, though all her friends had told me they were definitely coming.

So I asked Albert, my fishing friend. He trudged forward, pulled out a sheet of paper, and read out the name. There was loud laughter. He'd pulled out the name of Lena, his own daughter-in-law. There were cries of what sounded like 'Cheat, cheat'. I managed to dig out a couple of Beatles postcards, so in the end all six winners got a little something.

The list of the most-mentioned Beatles songs was

surprising. I expected that 'Yesterday' would dominate, but it got only two mentions, along with 'While My Guitar Gently Weeps' and 'Abbey Road'. Also mentioned were 'Yellow Submarine', 'Hey Jude', 'Sergeant Pepper', 'Hard Day's Night', 'And I Love Her', 'Girl', 'Let It Be', 'Across the Universe', 'Eleanor Rigby', 'Back in the USSR'.

At least half of them had written their answers in English, giving very full replies, though some of the spelling was a bit weird, such as 'Hay Jack' and 'Lonely Harts'. But then my own English spelling is not much better. And I can't write in Russian.

F. ● ● ● Dad did his Beatles talk at 6.30 in the cinema. Helen and Alex went and Fatsima wanted to go, but I refused as I wanted to spend all the time I had on the beach.

Walked on the beach with Marsha, Dasher, Alex, and F after supper. Alex saw some of his many friends light a fire so he strolled over too and we all reluctantly sat down. 3 blokes and 2 girls, very jolly etc then 2 more boys came with music, steak, vodka, juice and enormous bags of Georgian bread as it was someone's birthday so they all mucked around gulping vodka and singing . . . left at 11.30 and arrived in room before M and H?! Dad had invited his little friends at 10 to the end of the pier to drink his quarter of a bottle of whisky and told them 'bring a bottle if you like'. He came back at 12 full of himself ● ● ●

My little farewell drinkies on the Solarium was a bit slow to start. I don't think people liked the idea of drinking in such a public place while it was still quite light. I should have made it later. There was no music at first, as I'd planned, because of a mix-up over Lorka's machine, and my meagre supply of booze looked a bit weedy, till people began arriving, bringing bottles.

Sasha was about the first to turn up. He looked rather doubtfully at the drink I'd laid out, such as it was. 'Don't worry, Sash,' I said. 'If the police raid us, I'll throw it in the sea.'

'No need for that,' said someone else. 'Just offer the police a drink, then you'll be OK.'

People also brought nuts, fruit and several Georgian delicacies such as a string of rubbery sweets which I didn't know what to do with. Lorka rather hung about, and I worried I'd been unfair to him, but I think he was just waiting for Flora and her gang to turn up, which they never did.

In the end it was quite jolly. I'd taken my two bottles of vinegar, just in case things got really desperate, and some brave soul drank one of them. At the end of the party, I emptied the other one into the sea. I hope that doesn't count as pollution.

M. • • • Hunt's talk apparently a great success. His impromptu party on the sundeck at 10 pm not so impressive – invited all these people to share ¼ bottle whisky and 1 bottle of white wine. Luckily his guests generously brought some with them. I talked mostly to Fyodor's mother, Julia – excellent English too – about the usual topics. She tried to convince me the shops were empty because they'd been emptied – 'people will eat meat every day and so we run out of meat because they take it all.' Oh yeah? And, as for fruit and veg, it's just a problem of distribution which is being put right. As for dissident writers, she thinks Solzhenitsyn a bad writer who wouldn't get published in Russia whatever his politics. I think she's the first Russian I've talked to who I felt I didn't make contact with. She's been to GB – shocked by

171

boys shouting and climbing on statues in Trafalgar Sq. and by people 'wearing their overcoats in art galleries – so rude'. She then pointed out all the stars that could be seen only in this part of the hemisphere – much safer topic. Poor Lorka was miserable 'cos he'd loaned H's Beatle tape to someone and H wanted it to play at the party – he does tend to forget Lorka isn't Jake (who'd just shout back at him) • • •

We made our final farewells on the steps of the hotel early next morning. We were the only people going that day, as they all stay the full twenty-four days, so I had not expected many people to be around, but as we sat waiting for the mini-bus to arrive, the lift doors kept on opening and more people appeared. There must have been at least twenty-five lined up, parents and teenagers. Most of Flora's friends brought her little farewell presents.

According to Margaret, when Thackeray got into this situation, having made lots of holiday friends, he used to say he was going on the Wednesday, then leave secretly on the Tuesday night, to avoid any emotional farewells. I can see his point, but it would be hurtful to sneak away, as everyone had been so kind, in every way. I think we were all sad to leave.

M. • • • Time for a last swim at 8.30 – it's been one of the best parts of the whole holiday. Then a quick appearance in the dining room – one of the worst parts – for measly tea, not even any brown/black bread. Quite an emotional farewell – real cluster of some 20 people saying goodbye and a sudden flurry of cards with addresses and requests to ring X, Y and Z in London for them. Nina had tears in her eyes and Lorka blushed – it was really so touching. Flora's little group of friends were particularly forlorn and

172

sweet. Most people know for sure they ain't gonna visit London so it *is* goodbye forever. A v. strange feeling – I have grown so fond of them • • •

F. • • • Glad to be going home, yet overwhelmed by the emotional goodbye. At least 20 people were standing outside the hotel to see the 'ole English family orf. Nina was almost in tears and F, Armeine, Sasher, Helen, Alex, Tatzia were all hanging around, promising to write. Very humbling for *moi*. I actually felt quite wierd, thinking I would probably never ever see any of them again, having grown quite close in such little time • • •

CHAPTER FOURTEEN
Farewell to Moscow

Until we got to Moscow Airport we didn't know which hotel we were going to stay in. It was going to be simply a twenty-four-hour stopover and we wished in a way we could have changed planes immediately and gone on direct to London. The flight from Sochi had been very pleasant, but we were all feeling exhausted.

We were loaded down with presents. Flora had the things from her friends, while Margaret had six linen napkins which Sasha had given us at the airport, promising he would get us invited to Leningrad next time. (But if they don't like the things we might write, and something is bound to offend, will the invite ever materialise?) I left Sasha with an explanation of the phrase "hush hush" which pleased him. He'd been stuck, translating an Agatha Christie story, and had failed to find it in his dictionary.

I'd also laden myself with freebies. In the departure lounge at Sochi there was a massive bookstall, with a large range of very glossy, well-printed books, in English, French, German and other languages. All free. Please take them. They were propaganda books, of course. There was one justifying Russia's action in Afghanistan with a

174

really catchy title. 'Fighters for the Faith? No, Hired Killers.'

Marina was waiting for us, such a familiar and welcoming figure, and she'd got a decent taxi driver for once. Her bad news was that we were to stay once again at the Ukraine. I'd fancied a change, just to see the inside of a different hotel, but it would make things easy, knowing our way around. It was a smaller suite, 382 on the third floor, without a piano this time, and at the front of the hotel, so it was noisier. Her good news was that Georgi had indeed invited us to dinner.

While Flora and Margaret rested, I went down to the Beriozka to stock up for the last time. I wanted a bottle of whisky to give Georgi, as a present for having us, and something for Marina. It was closed. Oh no. Here we go again. Bloody Moscow and bloody alcohol regulations. I stormed around and was told it was closed just for twenty-four hours, for stock-taking. Fat lot of good that was. They would all have to have propaganda books as presents.

I was told there was a good Beriozka in the Inter-continental block, where we'd had lunch with the British Embassy man. I got completely lost trying to find it, but then I'm rotten at directions. I ended up in a block with armed guards on the door. I then had a huge walk along the river to the right place, realising as I walked that I had no passport on me or proof of who I was, so I might not get into the Beriozka. But I marched in as if I was a resident, and the doorman let me through.

It contained the most luxurious foods and drinks I'd seen in Russia, loaded with smoked salmon, hams, cheeses, caviar, and all sorts of Western delicacies, all at very reasonable prices. It was full of Americans and Brits, residents no doubt, stocking up for the weekend, perhaps the duration.

Les gels screamed at me when I got home. Where have you been, why didn't you tell us you were going off across

Moscow, some Russian girl called Rita has been trying to get you.

I'd forgotten her. When I'd checked in, I'd rung a number given me by Vladimir, my friend from the beach in Pitsunda. I had to ask for Rita, he said. She was the secretary of a brand-new organisation – the Beatles Fan Club of Moscow.

I rang her straight back and suggested she came in the morning for a coffee in our hotel, thinking that would suit her best. From my experience, people who run fan clubs are usually secretaries or hairdressers, not the sort with lavish accommodation. In Moscow, people anyway are a bit embarrassed about their small flats. We'd still not been to Marina's, and it now looked unlikely. But Rita said no, I should come and see her, at her place, tomorrow morning.

So that was two events lined up for our last twenty-four hours in Russia. Georgi had been the most interesting of all the people we'd met in Pitsunda. While the idea of a Beatles Fan Club, in Moscow, was bizarre.

M. • • • Marina met us at 7 pm and took us to Georgi's. Wonderful vegetarian meal – Tanya had come back specially from the country to cook it. Tomato salad, cucumber salad and a delicious carrot/raisin salad all beautifully prepared and presented. Then a sort of ratatouille with marrow, and green beans and cheese, and cauliflower followed by a moist, shortbread sort of cake with redcurrants on the top: a triumph. Georgi is proud of his wife being a total hausfrau, and Sonia, his 13 yr old by his first marriage, actually referred to her as 'the fairy of the house making everyone happy'. Oh my gawd. She was a small, well scrubbed bright child who of course made Flora seem about 25. She spoke quite good English but in a speak-yr-weight voice. Made tremendous efforts – you could see the labour. Flora tried hard but was too tired really. Georgi was my genial host, but then had one or two diatribes – mainly against Western writers like H who innocently had asked 'Was Brezhnev corrupt?' We come here and ask damn fool questions that no one can answer and then make generalisations from it. Bobby Sands died when he was in GB, but *he* didn't come back and write bits about how we torture the Irish • • •

The argument, and sudden change of atmosphere, had been so sudden, that I was caught unawares. I'd just been repeating some of the things I'd heard at Pitsunda, to amuse him, when he started lashing out, saying it was typical of Western people to pick up bits of gossip and then make terrible assertions about Russia, which they could not possibly prove. What can you know about a country in three weeks?

Quite true, but then what can you know in thirty years? I quoted to him a well-known saying by the 1860s writer, Nikolai Nekrasov: 'You can't understand Russia with your brains, nor can you measure it. You have to believe it.' I'd got that from Sash that morning. I thought three weeks was enough to get at least a flavour. Anyway, I would like to hear him talk or write about his experiences of Britain and the West. We all would. Then others could write and correct any little mistakes, or give their opinions. That way we would all learn.

He then started several stories about how ungenerous British people were, but of course he would never say such a thing in public. He had twice spent a whole day with famous British writers, whom he was going to publish in Russia, and they had been so inhospitable. You rang up, and they wouldn't even come and fetch you in their car. 'I spent a whole day once with M . . . and all I got was a cup of tea. Another time I even had to give someone money to buy a newspaper, and I never got it back.' But,

177

when British writers come to Moscow, he goes out to the airport and picks them up. And despite the lack of food in the shops, compared with Britain, they always lay on a feast. How upsetting to realise we have an image for being mean.

'No wonder you are a rich country. You don't spend your money on other people.' I tried to explain that I didn't know the circumstances. We always laid on proper meals when any visitor came, but living in London was different from living in Moscow. Every day people are coming in and out. You could spend your whole life just entertaining friends and visitors. Rather a limp defence, but it was all I could think of.

He also didn't think much of British food. 'You have a lot more, and the shops are full, but it tastes lifeless. I bought some huge strawberries in London on my last visit, which looked lovely, but they were tasteless. In Russian homes, the food is good. We might not have such a variety, but the taste is better.'

I didn't argue with this, but I got his point. Beware generalising from a small specific. He also maintained he'd been bugged in London. I said I'd expected that in Moscow, but half as a joke, having read too many silly thrillers. 'I was in the Kennedy Hotel, you know that, for three months. For no reason, they suddenly made me change rooms. I know it was because they were going to bug me.' Hey ho.

'Only in Russia can you have real friends,' he said. 'In the West they smile and say have a good day, but they don't mean it. They don't care. In Russia, when we say it we mean it.'

Russians would confuse us with America all the time, I said. I'd found them ignorant about our National Health and other things. In fact, I thought in Britain we did have a nice balance of capitalism and socialism, without the excesses of either.

'But you *are* a capitalist country. "Buy cheap, sell high"

178

that is your aim. You are controlled by multi-national corporations, just like America. They make the big decisions, and ordinary people have no say, have little freedom, less than we have.'

I said that our Government had the final say, not the big companies, but Georgi just laughed. 'It's all money. Reagan versus Carter? What's the choice. Where's the freedom there? They are both backed by capitalists and big business. They're just the same.'

Things calmed down a bit after the dinner was over, when we sat down on some sofas and he put on some music. His flat was comfortable, if not as elegant as some of the previous ones we'd been in, but he had not long moved in and things were a bit bare. It was a fairly old block, but we were on the top floor, with good views of Moscow.

I brought the subject round to publishing, as there was much I still did not understand, thinking it would be a safer topic.

I asked him to explain why, with such a big demand for books, there was always such a short supply. So many people told me how they rush into bookshops and find that, even with a print run of 100,000, they've all gone. With my Beatles book, which he was going to publish next year, at least I hoped he still was, I'd already had people asking me to take their name and make sure they got a copy.

'Paper shortage, that's the simplest answer. I am rationed, as all Russian publishers are. I could for example, keep reprinting for ever a popular book, such as Agatha Christie. I would earn bonuses for that, but I would then use up my paper allowance. I do 100 titles a year at Raduga and my aim is to give Russian readers a snapshot of world literature. If a book from America sells very well, then fine, but I won't reprint, because I'll have a new one from Nigeria I want people to read. I prefer to do the exotic.'

I then mentioned censorship. How did that operate in publishing? I'd been told there were three areas that were dodgy – sex, state security secrets, anti-Soviet propaganda. Was there an in-house censor to keep an eye on these? Well, that started him off once again and he turned the music down while he harangued me.

I'd got the idea of Russian censorship all wrong. Of course he couldn't publish pornography, but what about the *Lady Chatterley* trial in England. That was just twenty years ago. Russia was not so far behind the West. And it was good not to be allowed to publish books which are racist or against other countries.

'No one tells me which books to publish. If I am considering an English novel, or a Danish novel, I decide. Who could do that for me? I have that freedom. If there is a pornographic passage in it, I *could* publish it, but then someone would write and complain, there would be an investigation, and I would lose months, valuable time, in my explanations, when I could be doing better things. So at present I don't publish anything I consider pornographic.'

There are no political prisoners that he knew of, and the ones who ended up abroad and wrote their memoirs were nobodies.

'I often wish that all dissidents would be allowed to leave. If I was the leader, I would let them go at once, if they don't like it here. I once said that to a British diplomat and he said, "Please, no, we would then get all your rubbish. Look what happened when the Americans let in the Cuban dissidents. They got all those druggies and criminals."'

There was then a dramatic interruption, before we could get into further arguments, well let's say discussions. After that first flare-up, it had been pretty amicable and enjoyable. Alarms started sounding, bells ringing and I could hear the pounding of heavy boots outside Georgi's flat. Not the sort of noise one would normally expect on the top floor.

Sonia and Flora ran to the window of the kitchen overlooking the street, and rushed back to say there was a fire. Both girls had suddenly come to life, having had to listen to me and Georgi grinding on for so long. We could all smell smoke, once the dining room door had been opened. Georgi laughed it off at first, refusing to believe there was any danger.

Tanya and I then went to the kitchen window and looked down and it was most dramatic. We were on the tenth floor but we could clearly see the street was full of people, with at least a hundred standing watching a fire brigade which was sending up a lone fireman on an enormous ladder into the sky. It moved nearer and nearer and we realised with horror he was aiming for us – coming to a halt at the next-door window. The fire was in the adjoining flat. No wonder we had smelt the smoke.

We opened the front door of Georgi's flat, onto the landing, and there, beside the lift, were ten huge firemen, hacking away at an iron door which led up on to the roof. They were obviously going to break into the next-door flat from above, and put out the fire, while the other fireman attacked it from the window with hoses. They looked like spacemen, or Everest climbers, with bulky masks and packs on their backs, all carrying picks, yet somehow old-fashioned. Their clumsy helmets were made of steel and shaped like shovels.

Flora and Sonia had disappeared so I went round the flat, just two rooms, plus the kitchen and bathroom. I couldn't see them. I went out into the corridor again, looked down the stair-well. Firemen were rushing up and down the stairs like Keystone Cops.

181

Georgi was still faintly amused by the whole drama, but not as much as previously, realising that, if the blaze wasn't stopped, there could well be danger, and probably a lot of damage to his flat.

The lift suddenly appeared, the gates rattled open, and there were Flora and Sonia. I screamed at Flora for having gone off without telling us. Didn't she know when there's a fire you should never use a lift?

They said the fire was under control, no need to get upset, and anyway our taxi had arrived, and was waiting for us outside. It was quite a relief to get out of the building. It had been very hot and smoky in Georgi's flat.

We stood in the street for a few moments watching the firemen, still fighting the fire. The crowd around the engines were completely silent, as if watching a movie, not a real-life drama. It was all very calm. There were walkie-talkies and firemen urgently getting equipment out, but there were no firebells going on the various machines. No press reporters or TV cameras had turned up. Perhaps they hadn't heard. Perhaps it was not allowed. I thought of my early days as a reporter in Manchester, all the press rushing round at such scenes, madly trying to get interviews and quotes, adding generally to the noise and commotion.

We made fond farewells with Tanya and Georgi, who was now slapping our backs, terribly affable, promising undying friendship, and a contract for my book. Margaret promised to send Tanya a cookery book. Sonia said she would write to Flora.

In the taxi, we discussed Georgi's sudden change of mood. One moment being funny and laid back about Russia, joining in himself and telling funny stories, and the next on his high horse, attacking us with the Party spiel.

'Did you notice,' said Margaret, 'that it was at the dining table that he started. When we sat down, and he put the music on, he was more normal, but he turned the music down when he attacked you again.'

I hadn't. Did she mean we could have been bugged? No, don't be dopey, I said. You're becoming as bad as Georgi. Typical Russian paranoia. It was all my fault. I should not have trotted out that silly remark about Brezhnev and the alleged corruption. How do I know anything about such things? He was quite right.

My final Russian encounter was bound to be on safer, less controversial grounds – the Beatles. Or so I hoped.

Vladimir, my journalist friend from Pitsunda, turned up to take me to Rita's, just in case I got lost, which was very good of him. It meant that Margaret and Marina and Flora were able to go off all morning on their own. We arranged to meet for our final lunch, one o'clock at the National Restaurant in Gorky Street.

I had no idea what to expect as Vladimir had given me no clues about Rita, not even her name, or her job, if any. I was amazed to arrive outside the smartest, most affluent flats I'd seen so far, older and more distinguished than any block lived in by writers. They had been King's Cross. This block was more like Kensington, a handsome, Victorian edifice.

Inside, her flat was equally smart, with very tasteful furnishings, antiques, paintings, the biggest and best appointed of any I had seen. Perhaps not quite as many antiques as in Dimitri's flat, and I could see no sign at all of any ikons, but far more spacious and luxurious.

Rita was aged about thirty-five, rather sombre-looking, tired around the eyes, wearing smart green dungarees. She lives with her parents, she explained, and it was their flat. She was divorced and had a twelve-year-old daughter called Zoya, who lived with her. 'She likes good pop

music, not people like Rod Stewart. She's a Beatles fan.'
Rita got out a photograph of her daughter, taken with a
background of Beatles photographs.

We were in a rather formal room, but in a corner there
was Rita's desk and personal possessions, like a very tidy
student's. I could make out a paperback copy of my book
on a shelf, plus photographs of George and John and Che
Guevara, who appeared to be her three main heroes. She
showed me a scrapbook she kept, everything published in
the Russian papers about the Beatles, going back to 1967.
There was only one English cutting, from the *Morning
Star*, the only English paper normally available in Moscow.

She was educated at one of the Moscow Pedagogical
Institutes where she studied Spanish and English. She first
heard the Beatles in 1964 when she was in Hungary with
her father. 'I saw them on television and there were all
these girls crying and I couldn't understand it. I said to
myself, what's all this stuff? I disliked them.

'Then in 1966, when I was again in Hungary with my
father, I bought one of their records and listened to them
properly. It was "Sergeant Pepper" and that made me
realise how good they were. That's still my favourite. It
captures the spirit of our generation.'

In May 1986, she got together with a group of her
friends, all Beatles fans, and decided to begin a Moscow
branch of the Beatles fan club, with her as the unofficial
secretary. She stressed the unofficial. Not because the
authorities would object. The Beatles are now, at long
last, OK people, after years of being an underground
phenomenon.

I suddenly remembered that a year ago, in London, a
Russian émigré had sent me the manuscript of a book she
had written, called *The Beatles in Russia*. The title had
surprised me as of course the Beatles were never there,
but it was a most interesting document, showing the effects
of the Beatles on Russian youth and culture, on music,

clothes, language and design. I'd sent it back with a brief note, suggesting some British publishers who might be interested, but holding out no hope, thinking it was far too esoteric for a British audience.

It turned out this lady was a friend of Rita's. They were all part of the Sixties' Beatles worship in Moscow. According to Rita, her friend, Irina Pond, has since had some of her stuff published. She keeps her in touch from London with any Beatles news.

'We had planned to have a big opening meeting of the Beatles Moscow Fan Club, and we worked out a programme. We have a text on their life story, using slides and bits of films and of course the music. We were going to do it in May, using a Moscow group called The Twins. They only play Beatles music, so of course we needed them there. But the drummer caught a cold and we had to cancel. We're now going to do it next month. Everybody in Moscow wants to be there.'

They have booked a new place called the Rock Laboratory, a workshop used by sixty of Moscow's pop groups, a place where they can play and work and try out new things, from Heavy Metal to folk. There is a director and he does censor certain groups and certain songs, but it is a huge move forward, when you consider the situation five years ago, when all rock and roll was frowned upon.

'There still are rows,' she said, rather sadly. 'Some authorities still believe all rock is subversive.'

She herself writes pop songs, she said, and has been in trouble for them. I presumed this must simply be a hobby, a part-time amusement with her friends, but she said no, she was a professional writer of pop song lyrics and was in the appropriate union, part of the dramatists union.

But can you make a living in Russia, writing pop songs?

'No,' she said, smiling. 'I make kopeks.' She then got out a few of her albums and pointed to her name on several of them. Lyric writer – Rita Pushkin. I asked if

185

she was related to the famous Pushkin, but she didn't know. It was a big family.

She used to write a lot of songs for one of Moscow's best known groups, Autograph. (They appeared from Moscow on the Geldof Live Aid show.) She'd finished with them now. She considers them too cold and unemotional in their music, though very professional. She now writes mainly for Carnival, especially their lead singer, Alex Barekyn, whom she much admires.

She estimates there are 120 full-time professional rock groups in the USSR, with the best-known being Autograph, Time Machine and Bravo, a new group. There is just one professional heavy metal group, Aria.

In the popular music field, the numbers are much greater, groups doing middle-of-the-road sort of music. Two of the most popular singers, both women, have been made People's Artists – Sophie Rotaru and Alla Pugacheva. I'd heard the famous Sophie on many occasions, in taxis and hotels, and thought she sounded good. Rita was not that impressed. She liked strong rock and roll, or music with more heart and message.

'It is a great time of change in Russian rock and roll. Because it was blocked in the past, it was very hard for groups to be heard or succeed. Now there are several excellent groups coming through, playing their own brand of rock, with a Russian sound.'

During the last two years she has noticed one remarkable change. For most of her life, young Russian people interested in pop music always went for Western originals, as that was clearly the best and most innovative, rather than the despised Russian cover versions of Western music.

'I should say that, in discos, most of the music played is still Western, but when people are listening at home, serious fans of rock music, who are following what's happening, I should say that it's now 50-50, between listening to Western and Russian rock. It's equal. That's a huge advance, in just a few years.'

I remarked on the number of individual photographs she had of George and John, yet none of Paul and Ringo. Did she not like them as much? No, it wasn't that. Just that she much preferred George and John.

'George was always in the shadows of John, but I became very interested in him when he started on Indian philosophy, and he began to come out of the shadows. George has an interesting mind construction and an interesting soul. He was not as successful at the beginning when he went on his own, but he began to express himself in his record "Wonderwall", and with "All Things Must Pass". I like George's brain.

'John is to us a rebel, with a great sense of humour. Our generation have got great sympathy for him. John has secrets in his lyrics. Everything he wrote had a double meaning, which of course makes it hard for us. Look at Double Fantasy. That's very interesting. I know lots of my friends who have translated it into Russian, and everyone has got a different translation. No two are the same. John has something of Lewis Carroll in him.

'It was a terrible shock when he got killed. I didn't believe it. My friend who works in a news agency phoned me at midnight on December 9 and said he'd seen the telex, seen it on AP and UPI. It was some time before it was put out on the Russian radio, but by that time all my friends knew. Everybody was ringing everybody to tell the tragic news. It took five hours for the official announcement in our press, but by then everybody had heard the news.'

She then got out a tape, a demonstration tape, not a commercial one, of a song about the Beatles which she's written for Carnival to perform. It's called 'We listen to the Beatles.' So far, the authorities had not allowed it to be officially on sale. She didn't know why. You often could not work out what it was they objected to. For example, Beatle albums were now generally on sale in Russia, though you had to queue and be very quick, but for some reason, on the Russian album of Hard Day's Night, the track 'When I Get Home' had been omitted. There were worse tracks, with reference to drugs, which had got through. She shrugged her shoulders. You just had to wait, keep hoping. Perhaps one day her song would be available. You have to admit, she said, things are getting better all the time.

She then played her song, rather serious and mournful, but with a nice gentle rocking background. I got her to translate the words:

Whether the sunshine was dancing,
Whether the rain was working hard,
It made no difference to us,
We listened to the Beatles.
And the rainbow coloured walrus and his
Friends were knocking at our window.

Chorus: Oh we listened to the Beatles,
            Oh we listened to the Beatles,
            Oh we listened to the Beatles at that time.

The fool on the hill was inviting us for tea
And Lucy was descending from the skies
Everything was like a happening,
But our parents did not believe in the miracle
    of it all.

Chorus

And the silver hammer came down
Upon the heads of the nails imagined by John
We were starving for music and news.
From far away on the flowery roads
The Lonely Hearts Club was opening.

Chorus

Why should we remember all that?
Why should we remember all that?
Then someone calls us on the phone at midnight,
And asks us to tell them the words.

Chorus

And now in the office when we're not occupied
We hear the sound of what seems like guitars
    singing
And we fix securely to the walls around us
The portraits of Paul, George, Ringo and John.

I gave a lone clap. I thought it was terrific. Such a shame it could not be heard in Russian – because it was obviously a Russian song, in a Russian style, despite the content. She'd written the words first, then her friend in the group had put music to it. They'd recorded it in a private studio. 'It's meant to be in the style of Sergeant Pepper, using the same sort of instruments.'

She was clearly a serious Beatles fan, interested in the words and music, not trivia about their lifestyle, which was a refreshing change. She had obviously studied their music, just as PhD. students are now doing in Britain and America, and seen themes and patterns. The conversation never got round to what is Yoko really like, or are Paul and Linda happy.

She hasn't got a great deal of research material, or memorabilia, apart from a few British records, photographs and books. She would like more, if she could get any. She gave me the name of a real Beatles freak I should visit one day in Leningrad. He has turned his whole flat into a Beatles museum. I would be amazed by it.

She showed me round the rest of the flat. The next room was an even larger, most imposing room, with

189

drapes and posh sofas, but no signs of any Beatles stuff. This was obviously her parents' room.

I asked what her father did, which I'd wanted to ask earlier, but it didn't seem appropriate. She said he was in the army. Not the sort of Dad, perhaps, to approve of all this pop music and Beatles worship? 'Oh, he's always been very liberal. In the Sixties, when we were all young, he brought back a guitar for one of my friends.'

I thanked her for all her time, and the coffee and biscuits which she had provided. I gave her my last copy of *Beatles Monthly*, plus a photo of John, and promised to keep in touch.

On the way to the Metro, walking with Vladimir, who had agreed to take me in person to the restaurant where Margaret and Flora were waiting, I asked him what sort of soldier her dad was. Must be pretty high up, to have such a smart home.

General Pushkin, he said, Anatoly Pushkin, a very well known Russian officer, a Hero of the Soviet Union no less.

My, my, I said, that explains the affluence, and perhaps why she's been allowed to mix in underground rock and roll circles, full of people the authorities must have thought of as undesirables.

Vladimir paused and thought. It wasn't necessarily an asset. It could be a handicap in some ways. She had to be sure of people she met, just in case. They could be after her friendship for the wrong reasons.

He stopped and looked at me, half smiling, but I could see for a moment a worrying thought had suddenly struck him.

'*You're* not a spy, are you?'

I burst out laughing, denying it vehemently. Though, on reflection, I suppose that any Westerner, going into Russia and writing down things in his little notebook, which I did openly everywhere, is a spy of a sort.

I could of course have been a real one. I could have planted a bug in General Pushkin's private apartment. I even had his private phone number. It all had happened by chance, that first meeting on the beach with Vladimir. His mention of Rita, suggesting I should ring her. How trusting of them. I was touched by their openness and faith, but then worried, as I had been since arriving in Russia, that something I might write could land them in trouble.

M. • • • While Hunt went to see his Beatles Fan Club sec, Marina took me and Flora to another little park – not much bigger than Bedford Sq. with a pool in the middle, lots of trees, in an old part of Moscow. Lots of young dads pushing prams, little children playing in sand, etc – shades of the Heath. Then on to Red Square to see the guard change on the entrance to Lenin's tomb – only 3 soldiers, in dark green, who goose-stepped, flinging right arms across their chest – nothing to *our* changing of the guard sez I to Marina. Walked around Red Sq. a bit, Flora moaning, then couldn't get into Kremlin gardens – inexplicably closed like so much in Russia – so sat in front of the Univ. building. Then to lunch at the National – tomato salad, red caviar, and a crab delicacy M insisted on. Hunter didn't arrive till 1.20 – M slightly alarmed 'cos she hadn't taken his telephone number. He'd had a great morning – Vladimir, the journalist from Pitsunda, also there and brought him a Russian Beatles record.

Back to the Ukraine to check out – Sonia waiting with a doll (!) for Flora and a little dish for *moi*. Away in good time – traffic jam, but arrived in time. Marina did her last pushy act getting us thro' customs, etc – such bliss just following like little lambs. Tried to persuade the passport man to give us our visas as a memento: no go. Tried to get at least a Russian stamp on our passports: no go. How clean the airport is – and empty. A German crowd sitting beside us cheered when their flight was announced – I felt indignant on behalf of the Russians. Why should leaving Russia be a cause for cheering? • • •

F. • • • Now to sum up Moscow.

BUILDINGS: most are creamy yellow and quite pretty despite being box-shaped. Foreign-built buildings (e.g. Amer. Emb.) look much moderner. Lots of boring white/greyish tower blocks, as everyone lives in flats. A few golden and coloured domed buildings, like the Kremlin, which stand out in beauty from the square buildings. That was a surprise.

Hardly any public advertisements anywhere or decorations which make most streets look very bare.

Walking in many parts of Moscow you feel you could be in almost any European town, not in the hidden city of the KGB and commy spies.

Less policing than I expected. They often wait on the odd corner with walkie-talkies and uniform, but not fierce, daunting or suspicious of you, just going about their job in a vague manner.

PEOPLE: most are just as expected, especially the old women who could be nothing but Russian in their headscarfs, thick socks and boots, men's cardigans and other recognisable trade marks.

The clothes of young women and girls are not exactly '40s but slightly '70s with flower power just coming in, thick heels with socks, nylon frilly shirts and a point of making everything over-tight, especially tops.

Men's clothes are grey, too large, ugly and just drab and BORING.

I seem to feel staring, just staring, but if I made a point of smiling or nodding, there was no response. Most people look the other way, with only a few daring to smile back. (But if you smile at a stranger in London, would you get a pleasant response?) • • •

I can't actually think of anything 'secret' that anyone said to me in Russia, which is why I've changed no names, moved nothing around, reported what I personally thought I saw and heard and observed in those three short weeks. Russia is a free country, so they kept on telling me, as long as you don't attack the fabric of their society or stir up subversive activities. Nobody did that. They were totally loyal, give or take a few criticisms of economic conditions.

We were of course seeing only the best, the chosen few, the officially recognised writers, not a load of underground dissidents whose identity has to be disguised, judging by most books on Russia I have read. Should I change the names? That would be a shame. When Fyodor does win his Nobel Prize, you'll never believe I met him. Or when Rita Pushkin gets her Grammy award I'll be able to say you read about her first, right here.

I hope there will be no repercussions, some minor comment or observation of my own being blamed on someone else. Ah well. I apologise to them all in advance.

CHAPTER FIFTEEN

Three Months Later

Since we got back, we've had two surprise visits from Russians. You can imagine our panic to do the right thing and disprove their image of the Brits as being unfriendly and mean. We had of course given our address and phone number to lots of people, not thinking any of them would ever appear, but a week after we got back Dimitri Zhukov, the biographer and writer, turned up, over here to research his biography of Sir Thomas More. He'd been the previous day to the home of a famous historian of the Tudor period who in seven hours of chat had not given him a bite to eat. Ah well. We gave him a big lunch, and then tea, and I drove him round various local sites, such as Karl Marx's grave, Keats's house, Kenwood, Highgate.

He was most fascinated by Camden Lock, the stalls, clothes, fashions, music. Secondly, the cars. 'How do you choose a car?' he said, as we drove through town. The idea of having hundreds of makes and models and styles amazed him. In the end he pointed to the one he would choose as a Brit – a Range Rover.

Then a month later Albert Ivanov, my fishing friend from Pitsunda, rang up, over here with a party of thirty

Russian writers, doing the sights. He came for tea, with a friend, and solemnly gave us copies of his books. I asked him to take back some letters and photographs for our Russian friends. I'd already put them in envelopes, and stuck Russian stamps on. All very simple. But he and his friend became very agitated. He got out his dictionary and pointed to the word 'prohibited'. He would take letters, or the photographs, but not both in the same envelope. What a palaver. I wish I hadn't asked.

This problem of correspondence besets all people wanting to keep contact with Russian friends. Every guide-book warns about it, not to expect to hear anything ever again. We were told while in Russia that our postcards home would never get here for months, if at all, which turned out to be an absolute lie. Every postcard we sent home, from Moscow and Pitsunda, was here in five days – twice as fast as it takes from Portugal.

We have sent cards and letters, plus the photographs, to at least a dozen people since our return, but so far we have had only three letters in return. Fatsima, Flora's friend in Tashkent, has twice written, registering her letters, which must have cost a fortune. I have had a letter from Rita, giving me a better translation of her Beatles song, asking me to use it, not the one she did as we were sitting talking in her home. I've also had a beautifully-typed letter from Fyodor, thanking me for a Beatles book. Not a word yet from Marina, our bestest friend, despite several letters to her. Rather puzzling.

Despite the lack of letters, Russia has continually been in our thoughts. California, which we also visited that year, went completely from our minds, almost the moment we got back. So many things we encountered were part of the stereotype, the long queues, the rotten food, nothing in the shops, and people here nod their head and say yes, we have heard, but then I say these things don't really matter. It's people that matter. And, from what we saw,

195

the individual people could not have been friendlier or more decent. Were we conned, the wool pulled over naive eyes? I choose to think not, but it was only our personal experience.

On the whole, from my brief experience of each great country in the last year, three weeks in each, I would say the ordinary Russian is more peace-loving than the ordinary American. They don't react by screaming kill the Yankee bastards, determined to flex their muscles to show how strong they are. They just get saddened when they realise that Americans don't believe they are genuine about peace. The people I spoke to were amazed to be told that anyone can look upon Russians as frightening people. *They* are the ones who feel frightened: tender, sensitive souls that they are, so easily upset by any criticism, unable to understand why any Westerner should be horrible about them.

Russia's public face is far less attractive. Their brutal history, past and present, has warped them, encouraged their paranoia, made them far too suspicious of strangers. Then of course the last war still clouds all their thinking. It will be interesting to see what happens when a new generation is in power, who have grown up in forty years of relative peace and security. So many of their elderly leaders, in politics and the arts, remember their own wartime experiences, and react accordingly.

The Americans and the Russians have acquired such extreme images of each other, which the man in Gorky Street or on Broadway generally accepts. In Russia, it's assumed there's no freedom, just awful repression. America is believed to be decadent and money-mad. Both correct, as far as it goes, and you can easily get evidence to prove either. But it's almost as if each Government *wants* to keep up these extreme, unfair views, for their own purposes, to justify their own actions.

The Russians don't help with their silly restrictions and

censorship, especially of their own people. As Georgi said, they should let any dissident go at once. And also come back again, if they don't like it there, which many of them don't, missing Mother Russia. It's vital for more and more ordinary travellers to be able to move between, freely and informally, as we did. Since we got back, the poet Irina Ratushinskaya has been released, and managed to keep her Russian citizenship.

I think the most important single thing I learned in Russia was that the Russians don't want to leave. Despite everything, and they know the problems more than we do, they like it there. They won't all flock out, once the gates are open. So what are the authorities scared of? The more we know each other, the more we know ourselves, the less likely misunderstandings will happen. By keeping their own people in the dark, they are building up trouble, when there is little need to.

It is in their history, of course, long before Communism, this control of the populace, going back to Tsarist days. They are frightened of the outside, that their enemies are encroaching, and of their own vast country, that enemies within will seize power, if they are not kept in line. It's an insult to their own good citizens.

But things are changing rapidly, as everyone in Russia told us. They are coming out of their hard-lined shell, taking a few chances, being more open, in so many ways. Inviting us to meet informally 500 of their writers and families, with no strings attached. That *was* a chance. I hope they won't regret it. We certainly didn't.